THE STRAWBERRY GIRLS

THE STRAWBERRY GIRLS

BY HELEN MILECETE DUFFUS

INTRODUCTION BY
JANET B. FRISKNEY

FORMAC PUBLISHING COMPANY LIMITED
HALIFAX

Formac Publishing Company Limited recognizes the support of the
Province of Nova Scotia through the Department of Communities,
Culture and Heritage. We are pleased to work in partnership with
the Culture Division to develop and promote our culture resources
for all Nova Scotians. We acknowledge the support of the Canada
Council for the Arts which last year invested $24.3 million in writing
and publishing throughout Canada. We acknowledge the financial
support of the Government of Canada through the Canada Book
Fund for our publishing activities.

NOVA SCOTIA
Tourism, Culture and Heritage

The Canada Council | Le Conseil des Arts
for the Arts | du Canada

Canadä

Cover illustration by Saville Lumley
Author image from "The Favourite Corner" by Frances (Jones)
Bannerman, courtesy of Nova Scotia Archives.

Library and Archives Canada Cataloguing in Publication

Duffus, Helen Milecete, 1868-1936
    The Strawberry girls / Helen Milecete Duffus ; introduction by
Janet B. Friskney.

(Formac fiction treasures)
Includes bibliographical references.
Issued also in electronic formats.
ISBN 978-1-4595-0070-9

    I. Title. II. Series: Formac fiction treasures

PS8457.U34S73 2012   C813'.52   C2012-903518-1

Formac Publishing Company Limited
5502 Atlantic Street
Halifax, Nova Scotia, Canada
B3H 1G4
www.formac.ca

Printed and bound in Canada.

PRESENTING FORMAC FICTION TREASURES

Series Editor: Gwendolyn Davies

A taste for reading popular fiction expanded in the nineteenth century with the mass marketing of books and magazines. People read rousing adventure stories aloud at night around the fireside; they bought entertaining romances to read while travelling on trains and curled up with the latest serial novel in their leisure moments. Novelists were important cultural figures, with devotees who eagerly awaited their next work.

Among the many successful popular English language novelists of the late 19th and early 20th centuries were a group of Maritimers who found, in their own education, travel and sense of history, events and characters capable of entertaining readers on both sides of the Atlantic. They emerged from well-established communities that valued education and culture, for women as well as men. Faced with limited publishing opportunities in the Maritimes, successful writers sought magazine and book publishers in the major cultural centres: New York, Boston, Philadelphia, London and sometimes Montreal and Toronto. They often enjoyed much success with readers at home, but the best of these writers found large audiences across Canada and in the United States and Great Britain.

The Formac Fiction Treasures series is aimed at offering contemporary readers access to books that were successful, often huge bestsellers in their time, but which are now little known and often hard to find. The authors and titles selected are chosen first of all as enjoyable to read, and secondly for the light they shine on historical events and on attitudes and views of the culture from which they emerged. These complete original texts reflect values that are sometimes in conflict with those of today: for example, racism is often evident, and bluntly expressed. This collection of novels is offered as a step towards rediscovering a surprisingly diverse and not nearly well enough known popular cultural heritage of the Maritime provinces and of Canada.

Helen Milecete Duffus

INTRODUCTION

Welcome to the village of Happy Valley, New York, and the world of the Addington family: Mary, a widow in her mid-30s; her two teenage daughters, Lil, seventeen, and Nan, fifteen; and her much younger son, Billy, seven. A novel set contemporary to the time of its original publication in the early 1920s, *The Strawberry Girls* by Helen Milecete Duffus (1868–1936) offers a glimpse into New York society during a decade in which the US in general was in recovery from the sequential horrors of the First World War and the Spanish Influenza outbreak of 1918–19, a pandemic that killed millions worldwide. While neither of these catastrophic events is explicitly referenced in the novel — perhaps because readers of the time would have required no reminding — either one of them might have been the cause of the death of Mary's husband, an event about which we are offered no detail other than it occurred when Billy was very young.

Yet it was a profoundly significant event in the life of the family, economically as well as emotionally, for Bill Addington's death was clearly the catalyst behind the straitened financial circumstances under which we find the family operating when the novel opens. It's also a puzzling situation since both Mary and her husband clearly came from affluent backgrounds. Yet, upon Bill Addington's death, his widow and children appear to have been left with nothing but the modest house and land in Happy Valley which belong to Mary. It is from these, and with the help of her daughters, the daily man-of-all-work, Wood, and the faithful cook, Rose, that she has managed to make a sufficient living by growing and selling strawberries and vegetables to the local grocer, as well as to the wealthy New Yorkers who maintain summer homes in the nearby village. The drama of the novel emerges out of a series of trials — including a mysterious illness from which she is silently suffering — that threaten the hard-won equilibrium Mary has managed to achieve in the years since her husband's death.

The Strawberry Girls first appeared in a serialized version in *The Youth's Companion* of Boston between December 14, 1922 and February 15, 1923. By the 1920s, this weekly magazine, despite its name, targeted a readership of adults as well as children, and so stories like *The Strawberry Girls* would have been accepted — and quite likely deliberately written — with such a combined readership in view. As a venue, *The Youth's Companion* had an established reputation for publishing works by Canadian authors, among them Sara Jeannette Duncan, Isabel Ecclestone Mackay, Marjorie Pickthall, Charles G. D. Roberts, Ernest Thompson Seton, E. W. Thomson and Ethelwyn Wetherald. For a Nova Scotia-born writer like Helen Duffus, enduring links between the Maritime provinces of Canada and the New England states of the US may have been another influential factor in her decision to approach a Boston-based publication as a home for her story. Certainly Maritime contemporaries of Duffus often did the same, perhaps the most prominent among them being L. M. Montgomery of Prince Edward Island, who, in 1908, had published her well-known and enduring novel *Anne of Green Gables* with L. C. Page of Boston.

The text presented in this Formac Fiction Treasures edition is a reproduction of the book version of *The Strawberry Girls* issued by Jarrolds and Sons of London, UK, in 1923. While the characters and essential story of the book version remain consistent with the earlier serial version of the story, the Jarrolds edition of the work exhibits numerous textual differences, including changes in chapter breaks[1] and an expansion of the work as a whole. As readers, we can enjoy speculating about which changes to ascribe to Duffus versus those of her editors. Is it the case that book publication provided Duffus with an opportunity to restore a longer version of the work, one that had been cut down by editors at *The Youth's Companion* when the text was prepared for serial publication? Or, alternatively, did book publication offer the author the chance to revise and lengthen the manuscript she had originally written for serial publication? Intermittent substitution of words and frequent changes to the structure of individual sentences are certainly interventions that could be attributed to an editor at Jarrolds; however, the substantive additions of the occasional sentence or paragraph, as well as two whole chapters ("The Way Out" and "I'd Love Ten Dollars"), seem more likely to have been instigated by the author. A mixture of authorial and editorial intervention in advance of the book's issue in London is equally feasible.

When *The Strawberry Girls* appeared again in 1929, this time issued in the US by the New York City book publisher Duffield and Company, the text of the 1923 UK edition served as the base. Although the 1929 edition was newly typeset, only modest changes were made to correct errors in punctuation or typographical slip-ups in spelling. One change that might have been anticipated — a shift to American spelling for words like "colour" and "neighbour" — was not executed by the US firm.

The author of *The Strawberry Girls*, Helen Milecete Duffus, may be a stranger to many readers. Born Helen Wiseman Morrow in Halifax, Nova Scotia, Canada, on February 28, 1868, she was the daughter of Robert Morrow and his wife, Helen Stairs, both of whom came from prominent merchant families based in Halifax. As a result, Helen Wiseman Morrow and her siblings — one of whom was another Canadian-born fiction writer, Susan (Morrow) Jones — grew up under financially privileged circumstances on an estate called Birchham located on the city's Northwest Arm, a Halifax neighbourhood known for the wealth of its inhabitants. As literary scholar Gwendolyn Davies has related elsewhere, Helen Duffus and Susan (Morrow) Jones represented half of a significantly creative family quartet that was completed by their older first cousins (and childhood next-door-neighbours), Alice Jones and Frances (Jones) Bannerman.[2] Alice Jones distinguished herself as a travel writer and novelist while Frances Bannerman became a painter of international note. The young woman featured reading a book in Bannerman's work *The Conservatory* is possibly her cousin Helen as a teenager.[3]

Helen Duffus grew up in Halifax, but in 1889, at the age of twenty-one, she married Gordon Henry Paske (1862–1905), an officer in the Royal Engineers, a branch of the British Army which maintained a presence in Halifax well after Canada's Confederation in 1867. Within a year of their marriage, the couple moved to England, where their only child, Edward Lake Paske (1890–1971), was born in Clifton, Gloucestershire in April 1890. Precisely when Helen Duffus launched her literary career remains unclear, but in the UK Census of 1901, she identified herself as an "authoress." By that time, she was also living in London, with one female servant, while her son attended boarding school in Surrey, the county where her mother- and father-in-law resided. Her husband's name did not appear in the UK census of that year (he may have simply been away on military service). When Paske died in 1905, it was in Dorsetshire rather than London. A little over a year later, Helen was married in London to Edward John Duffus (1866–1937), a Halifax-born officer in the Royal Artillery who appears also to have been her second cousin.[4] While the UK seems to have been the couple's primary residence, surviving passenger lists reveal they took at least one trip back to Canada in late 1913. Helen Duffus died in England on April 29, 1936, predeceasing her second husband by about eighteen months.

Pinning down the literary legacy of Helen Wiseman Paske Duffus is difficult. An obituary published in Halifax stated she "was well known as a writer of short stories and several books."[5] However, the "Helen Milecete" pseudonym is one that was also used by her sister, Susan (Morrow) Jones, and investigation by Canadian literary scholar Gwendolyn Davies suggest that much of the writing done under that name was executed by Susan.[6] *The Strawberry Girls*, however, is one title that has been clearly associated with Helen: in both serial and book editions of the work, the full name of the author was given as "Helen Milecete Duffus" or "Helen Milicete Duffus," and Davies has further confirmed Helen Duffus's authorship through discovery of a handwritten attribution contained in a copy of the book held by a member of the author's extended family.[7] Davies and her fellow Canadian literary critic Carole Gerson also believe that a second novel, *The Career of Mrs. Osborne*, was likely co-authored by Helen Duffus in collaboration with her sister, Susan. When the story first appeared in a serialized version in *The Smart Set* in 1901, the authorship was given as "S. Carleton and Helen Milecete" while the book version of 1903 appeared under the authorship of "Carleton-Milecete."[8]

Readers familiar with the popular and enduring American novel *Little Women* by Louisa May Alcott, which features the four March sisters, Meg, Jo, Beth and Amy, may find a certain resonance between that work and *The Strawberry*

Girls. Published originally in two parts in 1868 and 1869, and frequently reprinted after that, *Little Women* was a novel with which Helen Duffus was more than likely familiar. Her inclusion in *The Strawberry Girls* of a family called "Marsh" as secondary characters — a name only one letter removed from "March" — may even have been a playful allusion to the influence of Alcott's book. At any rate, one can certainly draw parallels between the first part of *Little Women*, which follows a year in the life of the March family and ends with Meg's engagement to Brooke; and the story recounted in *The Strawberry Girls*, which begins in the summer strawberry season when the two Addington sisters, Lil and Nan, are seventeen and fifteen respectively — a close approximation of Meg and Jo's initial ages — and closes about half a year later, a few weeks past American Thanksgiving, with the announcement of Lil's engagement. Like Jo in *Little Women*, Nan responds to the news of her sister's engagement with resignation rather than joy, not for any dislike of her future brother-in-law, but because the marriage of her sister will mark the end of a particular era in their lives as a family.

What other parallels between *Little Women* and *The Strawberry Girls* might we draw? Perhaps the most obvious one is that of a genteel family committed to maintaining its respectability in the face of reduced financial circumstances, not too proud to engage in honest work for the vital income it brings, but nevertheless firm in recognizing that certain social boundaries cannot be transgressed without loss of reputation. For instance, Lil and Nan must harvest strawberries and vegetables from the family garden, but are prohibited from delivering the produce to the back doors of their clientele. The latter work remains under the purview of the family's man-of-all-work. In terms of characters, a marked resemblance exists between Jo of *Little Women* and Nan of *The Strawberry Girls*. Though less tempestuous than Jo in her overall character, Nan is nonetheless similar in the way she disregards her appearance, embraces "tomboyish" ways, works hard, consumes books, enjoys sailing, sports a quirky hat and loves her family profoundly. By contrast, Lil seems more a composite of Meg and Amy and, like them, emerges as much more self-conscious of the family's loss of financial consequence and the social slights that accompany that change of status. In both books, the mothers of the household are held up as ideals of respectable womanhood. As Cousin Adelaide advises Lil: "My dear, model yourself and your style on your mother — the most perfect gentlewoman I have ever met." Since Adelaide is the widow of a son of a British earl, her words carry weight. Finally, the practical and kindly interventions into the lives of the Addington family by Adelaide — as well as by Mr. Perry Earlwood — may remind readers of the generosity toward the March family exhibited by the characters Mr. Laurence and Aunt Carrol in *Little Women*.

Whatever inspiration Helen Duffus might have drawn from Alcott's novel, *The Strawberry Girls* merits attention for its own sake. At one level, the book unfolds simply as a very cheerful and engaging read. Indeed, the reader becomes caught up in the simple pleasures of the Addington family, and, in particular, the antics of young Billy, whose adventures over the course of the novel lead, among other things, to the inadvertent capture of Mr. Yelverton in his fishing line and the deliberate incarceration of the music teacher, Herr Schneider, in the harness-room. Billy's powers of persuasion are also such that, by chapter four, he has his adult and very proper Cousin Adelaide crawling along the floor behind him in a white, embroidered dress as they co-investigate the activities of the family's dogs.

Billy's escapades serve as comic relief to more serious issues explored in *The Strawberry Girls*, such as the novel's

exposition that wealth and class are not synonymous, a theme
revealed predominantly through the foil of the neighbouring
Yelverton family, whose ill manners and excessive materialism
are critiqued throughout. As Mary Addington reflects early in
the novel, "Not one of them, from fat Mr. and Mrs. Yelverton
down to Tony home from Yale, Nettie the schoolgirl, and
Tommy the spoilt small boy, had one thought in the world
beyond money and their own sweet wills." The sense of
entitlement that wealth imbues in all members of the Yelverton
family makes a decided impact on the Addingtons because
of the regular interaction between the two households, and
particularly between the children. As the story opens, Lil has
become discontented with her lot, due in large part to the
exposure to the material benefits of wealth revealed to her
by Nettie. While in general far more insightful than Lil about
the pretensions of the Yelvertons, Nan too proves suscept-
ible to Nettie's influence over the matter of a dance costume,
the materials for which Mrs. Addington is forced to deny her
daughter — an outcome, it turns out, that Nettie anticipated.
Nan also falls victim to young Tommy Yelverton, who, after
Nan calls him a "nasty little boy" for treating one of Billy's
dogs cruelly, responds with a vengeful act that has significant
financial repercussions for the whole Addington family.

    The most menacing influence emanating from the Yelverton
household is Tony, the college-aged son who, in Mrs.
Addington's view, "had brought nothing from Yale but the
worst characteristics of its fastest set." Seventeen-year-old
Lil appeals to Tony, and she, in turn, is infatuated by him.
Through her fifteen-year-old eyes, Nan simply dislikes Tony
as a person, and considers him a snob. However, Mary
Addington and Cousin Adelaide clearly view Tony as a threat
to Lil, and Cousin Adelaide eventually sweeps Lil off to New
York City, where Lil is exposed to a better class of people (by

her mother and cousin's definition) and placed in a position
to find a wealthy but honourable young man who will marry
her despite her family's financial decline. Why would Tony have been considered such a threat? In
New York society in the 1920s, a young, single woman's virtue
still represented the cornerstone of her respectability. Virtue
supported a good marriage, and marriage was viewed as a key
ingredient in the financial security of many women's future.
Young women claiming a certain social status made a "debut"
or "came out" into society. The debut was "the first formal
appearance in public of a young woman," one which "denoted
her sexual maturity and availability for marriage."⁹ In this
debut, as well as the social rounds that followed it, the young
woman would be guided and chaperoned by her mother or an
alternative woman designate in that role — in Lil's case, that
role is played by Cousin Adelaide, and her initial time in New
York is spent in preparations for the social ritual of the debut.
Some of the details of those preparations are revealed in Lil's
letter home, a piece of correspondence that also provides
insights into the general social and material world of New York
society during that era. Prior to Cousin Adelaide's intervention,
Lil was not in a financial or social position to make a debut
into society. Instead, her family's reduced circumstances left
her in a position of vulnerability to a "fast" young man like
Tony Yelverton, who might find a certain sport in romantic-
ally pursuing a woman in Lil's position to the point where her
respectability would be compromised, but after which no offer
of marriage would be forthcoming.

While there's the sense at the end of *The Strawberry Girls*
that Lil is about to be restored to the social world and financial security from which her father's untimely death cast her,
Nan's future trajectory remains ambiguous. On the one hand,
there are hints toward the end of the novel — most notably

in the chapter "Nan Blossoms Out" — that Nan's "tomboyish" aspect is beginning to give way to a nascent womanliness, one that in the not-too-distant future might bring her a husband and financial security such as Lil has achieved. On the other hand, Nan articulates a steady ambition to attend university, an action that would have set her apart from the majority of American women in the 1920s. Although some US colleges began to accept women after the American Civil War of the 1860s, in 1920 the proportion of women registered in US colleges stood only at about 7.5 per cent.[10] Post-secondary education of women remained a socially questionable pursuit in the eyes of many, in part because some construed it as a rejection of marriage in favour of spinsterhood and paid employment. Cousin Adelaide's initial reaction to Nan's ambition to attend university is certainly negative, though she comes round later. By contrast, the railroad magnate Perry Earlwood takes Nan's university ambitions seriously; indeed, he actively encourages her in the idea, and, through his intervention at the end of the novel, places the Addington family in a position where Nan's dream might be realized should she decide to pursue it.

Through the two strawberry girls, Lil and Nan, and their mother Mary, the author may be trying to tell us that choice and options are a fine thing for girls and women to have. Certainly Mary's economic struggles in the wake of her husband's death demonstrated to her daughters — and to the readers of *The Strawberry Girls* — that marriage and its promise of long-term financial security for a woman may be a terrible illusion; that, in fact, marriage sometimes represents only a discrete portion of a woman's life, and whether existing within or outside of that state, she may be thrown on her own resources to survive and prosper.

— Janet B. Friskney

ENDNOTES

1   "The changes in chapter titles in *The Youth's Companion*
    versus the 1923 Jarrolds edition are: Chapter One "Cousin
    Adelaide's Reception" becomes "'Happy Valley!'"; Chapter
    Two "The Pirates of the Cove" becomes Chapters Two and
    Three, respectively "The Engine" and "The Pirates of the
    Cove"; Chapter Three "Billy's Important Business" becomes
    Chapters Four and Five, respectively "Lil's New Dress" and
    "Billy the Jailer"; Chapter Four "Nan's Innings" becomes
    Chapter Six and part of Chapter Seven, respectively "Outside
    the Big Shoal" and "Lil's Party"; Chapter Five "Two Picnics
    in One Week" becomes the latter part of Chapter Seven
    and Chapter Eight, respectively "Lil's Party" and "He Can
    Swim"; Chapter Six becomes Chapters Eleven and Twelve,
    respectively "Theatricals" and "The Gold Thread"; Chapter
    Seven "The Blackberry Patch" becomes Chapters Thirteen
    and Fourteen, respectively "Cousin Adelaide Turns Fairy
    Godmother" and "Nan's Winter Suit"; Chapter Eight "Billy's
    Turkey" becomes Chapters Fifteen and Sixteen, respective-
    ly "Billy's Turkey" and "Nan Blossoms Out"; Chapter Nine
    "The Road to King's Palace" becomes Chapter Seventeen
    "Billy"; and Chapter Ten "Mother Comes Home" becomes
    Chapter Eighteen "Mother."
2   See Gwendolyn Davies, "Art, Fiction and Adventure: The
    Jones Sisters of Halifax," *Royal Nova Scotia Historical
    Society Journal,* 5 (2002): 1–22.
3   Davies, "Art, Fiction and Adventure,"4.
4   Genealogical materials available through various online
    sources suggest that Edward and Helen were second
    cousins through their respective grandparents, John
    Duffus and Mary Ann Morrow *née* Duffus, who were
    brother and sister, and themselves the children of William

Duffus and Susannah Murdoch.

5   Halifax Obituary, April 29, 1936, cited in Gwendolyn Davies, "Introduction," *A Detached Pirate: The Romance of Gay Vandeleur* by Helen Milecete. (1900). Formac Fiction Treasures. (Halifax: Formac, 2010), xv.

6   Davies, "Introduction," xiii–xvi.

7   Davies, "Introduction," xviii, note 19.

8   Carole Gerson, "Restoring Helen Morrow Paske Duffus (1868–1936)," *Canadian Notes & Queries* (1989), and Davies, "Introduction," xiv–xv.

9   Maureen E. Montgomery, *Displaying Women: Spectacles of Leisure in Edith Wharton's New York.* (New York: Routledge, 1998), 41.

10 This statistic appears in "Early College Women: Determined to Be Educated," a "Woman of Courage" profile produced by the St. Lawrence County, NY Branch of the American Association of University Women, and available at www.northnet.org/stlawrenceaauw/college.htm (Accessed March 26, 2012).

THE STRAWBERRY GIRLS

CHAPTER I

" HAPPY VALLEY ! "

NAN ADDINGTON was late for breakfast.
" Principally because I seem to have been up
ever since it stopped being night," she thought,
wrathfully. " I wish keeping a strawberry
garden didn't mean the strawberries in it had
to be *picked* ! " She threw down a strawberry-
stained overall, washed her obstinately-pink
fingers, and turned firmly from a chance glimpse
of her looking-glass and her untidy brown hair.
" I simply can't smell coffee and fuss with looks,
even if I am fifteen and ought to be neat," she
observed to the empty room where her elder
sister had dressed. " Lil will be neat enough
for two, anyway. Whew, breakfast, you smell
lovely ! "
With which she took the stairs in a running

jump, with one hand on the banisters, and burst
into the living-room.

"Oh, coffee, mother—quick!" she began,
and paused halfway between the door and the
breakfast table. The family sat at it just as
usual : Lil, seventeen and very pretty, with
the real corn-yellow hair and blue eyes people
always turned to look at ; small Billy, just
seven and the care and joy of his mother ; and
Mother herself. But Mrs. Addington was not
looking at all as usual. She was reading a
letter with a queer preoccupied look that quick-
eyed Nan knew was not all pleasure. "Mummy,
what is it—what's the matter ? " she cried.

Mrs. Addington raised her head.

"Nothing," she returned, hastily. " Except
—oh, Cousin Adelaide Sinclair wants to come
and make us a visit ! "

"Cousin *who* ? " Nan stared. She had
never heard of any Cousin Adelaide. Besides,
Mother, Lil, and herself, who ran a strawberry
garden, with vegetables for a side-issue, and
lived on what they could make off supplying
the tables of the summer visitors round the
village of Happy Valley, were not exactly prepared for any sort of cousin wanting to come
and stay. "I don't know who on earth the
cousin is," she observed, resignedly ; "but I

suppose she'll have to come if she wants to !
Only——"

" She can't," Lil cut in, blankly. " Besides,
who *is* she, mother ? We never heard of any
Cousin Adelaide Sinclair."

" She's Mrs. Sinclair, your father's cousin "
—disjointedly. " She has lived in England
ever since before you were born, but—this
summer she's been visiting the British
Ambassador's wife at Newport. I—oh, of
course I must let her come here ! "

" Here ? " Lil gasped. " Mother, you can't !
She's probably frightfully grand, with lovely
clothes, and we—why, we haven't even any
servant ! "

" There's Rose," put in the practical Nan.
Rose had been the cook when there was money
for a cook, but was living now with her old
mother in the village. " Rose will have to
come back and cook if Cousin Adelaide comes
here. I'd like to see one of her chicken salads
myself, too."

" Chicken salads," Lil interjected, scornfully.
" We'll have to have late dinner for a person
like Cousin Adelaide."

" We'll be just as we always are."

" And who'd wait if we did have dinner ? "
Mrs. Addington and Nan both spoke at once.

" Billy Boy, would you dress up in a black suit and change the plates ? " asked Nan.

Billy gave a solemn chuckle, " 'Spect I'd drop them ! " He got down from his chair, retrieved a small black dog, Doll by name, who had been waiting patiently under it, and prepared to go out.

" Wait, children, do," said Mrs. Addington, absently. " Do you realize, all of you, that Cousin Adelaide's coming *to-morrow* ? Lil, or Na—— No, I can't spare you girls ! Billy, will you run down to Rose's, and tell her Mother says will she come up to-morrow for a week ? "

" I was going fishing with Tommy Yelverton," Billy began, and Nan caught his eye.

" Run along to Rose's first," she cried. " You can fish afterwards ; I'll get your lines ready. Go on, Little Boy Blue ! "

" I love her name—Adelaide Sinclair." Lil looked admiringly at the signature of the note her mother had put down. " Who is she really, mother ? "

" She was Adelaide Addington, your father's cousin, who married an Englishman named Sinclair, a son of Lord Orderdale's. Her husband died some time ago, but during his lifetime Cousin Adelaide was a lady-in-waiting to the Queen of England."

" Then does she wear a crown ? " Billy turned hastily in the doorway.

" Of course not ; she isn't a queen." Nan rose from the table like a whirlwind. " Get on, Billy Boy, you caterpillar, and come quick, Lil," she exploded. " Let's get the garden work done and help mother.

Lil sat still.

" There are such tons of berries to be picked, and my hands do get so ugly," she wailed. " Mother, couldn't the old strawberries go just for to-day ? I'd much sooner help you with Cousin Adelaide's room."

Mrs. Addington shook her head. " Ripe strawberries wait for no girl ! Besides, the money for them has to keep us next winter."

" I never want to see a strawberry again." Lil grumbled.

" Oh, dear ! " Nan ran her hands through her brown hair till it was rougher than ever, and turned on Lil hotly. " Don't be piggy, Lil ! You know Mother couldn't even feed us if it weren't for strawberries ! "

" Well, it isn't nice for father's cousin to see us slaving at them "—crossly. " If she's so frightfully grand, and stays with ambassadors' wives, she'll despise us ! "

" Dear Lil," warned her mother, " if she did

despise us, what matter ? It would be she who
was horrid, not we."

"Well, I never heard of swell people having
a strawberry garden ! "

"Perhaps not ; but how do you suggest we
should live without it ?" Mrs. Addington was
worried. Lil had never grumbled before. "You
don't mean you're ashamed of it ? "

"Yes, I am "—slowly. "Mother, I've
always hated it—and I hate it more now,
with a Cousin Adelaide coming to look down
on us. I know she will ! Lots of girls do, when
I go to history class in the winter."

"You don't look at it the right way," returned
her mother, slowly. "But there's no time
to talk now. Mrs. Yelverton wants some
asparagus sent up at once."

"Then it won't be," Nan replied, promptly.
"I sold the last batch this morning. Mother,
do you know we've made nearly a hundred
dollars out of asparagus ? It's a mercy so many
rich families come here for the summer. Go on
about Cousin Adelaide—quick, mother !—before
I go out. Why didn't we know we had her ? "

"She lived abroad, and I had no time for
letters. I'd almost forgotten her till this
morning."

"She'll think this place dreadfully workaday

and untidy," Lil said, obstinately. " Besides, who's going to meet her at the station ? Our wagon has no paint on it, and old Jane, the pony, is a show ! "

" Why, Lil, dear, you must have a headache ! " Mrs. Addington really gasped it. Nan had moods, as she well knew ; but for the sweet and placid Lil to break out like this was unheard of.

But Lil had let all holds go. " Look at us," she sobbed. " Look at everything ! The garden, the house, all so dreadfully shabby ; and we work so—so hard ! "

" Why, Lil ! " But Mother said it with her hand on Lil's shoulder, and a nod to Nan to go. " My poor Lil, what is it ? "

" Everything "—chokingly. " Mother, you don't know how hard it is to be growing up, and having to do without everything other girls get ! "

" Don't I ? "—unexpectedly. " Only I didn't guess you felt it so bitterly. I was a girl myself once, Lil. Why, I was only eighteen when I was married. And that was hardly eighteen years ago."

" Why, then, you're only thirty-six ! " Lil gasped.

" And I feel one hundred, just from that

going without that worries you! Listen, Lil.
You can remember coming here after your
father's death, when I had no money and
nowhere else to go. This house and land
belonged to me, so I tried growing things, and
succeeded in a small sort of way. I never had
the capital to run the place properly. I feel sad
when I realize how you hate it, but what else
could I have done—or do now? And let me
tell you your cousin won't despise you, whatever
she does. You may be sure of that."

"I know," Lil confessed. "I was silly.
Only I felt discontented because—— Oh,
mother, I do so want to go to the dance Nettie
Yelverton's having next week, and I suppose I
can't. It's to be a real dance, with music from
New York. Nettie says I'd only need a simple
dress "—appealingly.

"Oh—Nettie!" said Mrs. Addington, slowly,
and with late enlightenment. So it was the
Yelvertons who were making Lil miserable!
And for the hundredth time Mrs. Addington
wished the Yelvertons had built their huge
house—which they called a bungalow regardless
of its four stories—anywhere but in Happy
Valley. It was not because they were rich—
plenty of richer people had houses along the
cool shore of the little Atlantic bay—but just

somehow, that they were the Yelvertons. Not one of them, from fat Mr. and Mrs. Yelverton down to Tony home from Yale, Nettie the schoolgirl, and Tommy the spoilt small boy, had one thought in the world beyond money and their own sweet wills. They were Mrs. Addington's best and most condescending customers; but they were, unfortunately, her nearest neighbours, too. Lil and Nettie were hand in glove; Tommy, being Billy's age, haunted the house unceasingly; and Tony— but Mrs. Addington was too wise to say aloud that Tony had brought nothing from Yale but the worst characteristics of its fastest set.

"Oh, mother, do say something!" Lil cried, impatiently. "I know you don't like Nettie much, but I do want to go to her dance. Couldn't I take some of the asparagus money for a dress?"

Mrs. Addington's face fell. "I'm afraid it wouldn't be fair. The others——"

"Nan never wants anything, and Billy's only a baby. Oh, mother——"

"Mummy!" Billy's voice, in a shriek like a syren, cut her off on the word. "Mummy, come quick—quick!" He yelled from the veranda. "He's going to be drowned!"

"Drowned? Heavens, he must mean

Tommy ! " Mrs. Addington was out on the veranda like a flash, with visions of the youngest Yelverton having been fishing with Billy, and lying now in the eelgrass of the bay. " Billy——" she exclaimed, and stopped short.

Whoever was going to be drowned it was obviously not Tommy Yelverton. He stood before her, calm and grinning ; and before him, Billy, with a very white, very woolly puppy clutched in his arms.

" It's him," he wailed. " Bob Burgess has got to drown him. His father says so—the man who helps us fish."

He nodded backwards, and Mrs. Addington was aware of yet another small boy—a very small one—leaning against the veranda railing, speechless with snuffly tears. " But why——" she began.

" His father says he won't have the pup round, and he told Bob to drown him. And, mother——"

" Can't drown him," burst in the snuffling Bob, but Billy never paused.

" Can't we keep him ? " he begged, wildly. " He's so woolly and little, and drowning is awful big for him."

" I don't know." Mrs. Addington hesitated. " You have Doll, Billy."

"Doll loves him"—promptly. "Oh, mother let me have him till I find a home for him anyway. He's so anxious, and he begs so. See!"

The woolly puppy licked Billy's hands frantically with a very pink tongue, and somehow Mrs. Addington's scruples fled.

"Very well," she agreed. "Only we'll call him the Boarder, Billy. And, remember, he's only going to stay with us—not coming to live."

But all terms were the same to Billy and Bob Burgess, who stopped crying, except in long gasps that shook what little there was of him. Lil watched her mother head a procession to bestow the new boarder in the back regions, and feed his late master with cake, before she joined Nan belatedly in her strawberry picking.

"Mother's as childish as Billy," she announced. "She's let him have a new puppy this morning. I wish she'd hire a man to pick these old berries instead!"

"She can't." Nan never even looked up. "Old Wood's all Mother can manage to pay, and he has enough to do with the cow, and driving old Jane to market with stuff. It's hard on you, because you care about your hands. I don't mind it much."

Lil sniffed. "Do you think Cousin Adelaide

will bring a maid ? " she demanded, suddenly.
" Mother's afraid she may, and that would be
too awful. I wish she wasn't coming at all ! "
" She may be nice "—rather doubtfully.
Lil shook her head. " Don't believe it. Oh,
Nan, I do so want to go to Nettie Yelverton's
party, and I know I can't." But a sudden
light flashed into her down-bent face. " Nan,
wouldn't it be splendid to send Cousin Adelaide
to it ?   Mother says she's the Honorable Mrs.
Sinclair, because her husband was the younger
son of an earl, and you know what the
Yelvertons are like.   Even if she's a horrid old
thing, wouldn't they be *impressed* ? "
" They might be "—absently.   " But I don't
care who goes to their old party so long as I
needn't.   I'd love it, if it were only boys and
girls, but I'd be terrified of the college men
Nettie's asked.   I suppose you'll like dancing
with them ? "
" How can I dance with them when you know
I can't go without a new dress to wear ?   And
Mother thinks I ought not to take any of the
asparagus money."
" You can have my piece of pink *crêpe* that
isn't made up."   Nan was always generous.
" I don't want it ; it's too fragile.   Oh, Lil,
don't pick those little berries !   Mother said we

could have them for to-morrow night. Frank
Marsh and the other boys are coming to the
Cove to camp, and I said we'd take our supper
over. We can get a good basket of little
strawberries, and some potatoes to roast, and
a corn-cake. I love corn-cake out of doors."

" I don't care much for boys' picnics now "
—crossly. " I—— Oh, Nan, I know I'm a
pig to complain, when you never do. But all
the girls my age are going to grown-up picnics
every day, and having a lovely time with all
the men from college ! "

" I know it's hard." Nan nodded sympa-
thetically. " Only I hope I won't get grown-up
soon. It doesn't seem to make you happy."

Lil winced with late remorse. " I'm happy
enough," she said, slowly. " Only sometimes
I do get cross and horrid. It's lucky that
Mother never does."

" Mother's looking awfully tired all the same "
—sharply. " She's working far too hard. I
asked her if she couldn't afford to have Rose
back this winter, and take a rest, but she said
she was afraid she couldn't. She wanted to
send you to all the winter classes this year,
and give you all the advantages she could."

" I didn't think of that," was all Lil said.
But at the dinner table she looked at her mother

in self-reproach and penitence for her wicked stupidity. Mother did look tired out, and she had never noticed it before. " Are you dreadfully tired, mother ? " she questioned, suddenly.

" A little "—rather faintly.

" Well, we'll clear up," said the cheerful Nan, " and you go and rest. Billy and I'll wash the dishes, and Lil's going to see that Wood gets off with the strawberries to Fielding the grocer."

" I think I will lie down, then "—slowly. " Only, if a telegram comes from Cousin Adelaide saying what train we're to meet to-morrow, one of you bring it to me to answer, will you ? "

" Is her room ready ? " Lil inquired, as Nan nodded.

" Yes, unless you can think of something else. Go and look at it, will you ? "

Lil did ; and added some treasure of her own to the dainty blue-and-white guest-room.

" It's pretty humble," she commented, disparagingly, to Nan.

But Nan shrugged her shoulders. " It's nice, and—— Oh, what does it matter anyway ? Come and get the dishes put away. Billy you put the Boarder out on the veranda with Doll, and bring the carpet sweeper."

But the Boarder refused to stay on the

veranda. Billy ran the sweeper, closely attended by both his dogs, till he could turn with a relieved sigh and disappear, leaving Nan to cast a last glance over the cleared-up room.

It was a shabby, cosy living-room, made pleasant in summer by a big veranda, on the south and west, whose doors were apt to be draughty in winter, and opening on a square hall lit by a long, low window; and it served for every purpose of the Addington family. They had no time to dust a useless parlour, and if the living-room furniture was worn its chairs were easy. There were plenty of tables—sturdy ones—where the girls could sew, and Billy paint gorgeously in old magazines and beat his sisters at "Animal Grab" in the evenings. Noise never disturbed Mrs. Addington, which was as well at that moment, for Billy's voice suddenly descended piercingly from the very top of the house.

"Nan, Tommy Yelverton's come to play, and I'm in the attic getting the things to dress up. You and Lil play too?"

"All right," Nan shrieked while she swept up the kitchen floor. She was banking the fire as Billy rushed in on her.

"Get ready," he commanded. "We'll play we're going to see the King of England. All the things are in the hall. Hurry and get your Court dress on ! ''

It was no hasty business, though Billy marshalled the Court ladies and directed operations ; but when all was done the scene was brilliant. Lil, wearing an old white satin gown of her mother's and a train draped out of a dilapidated red bed-quilt, looked beautiful in spite of feeling herself too grown-up for Billy's plays. Nan was in her element, with a feather duster rakishly disposed in her hair, and a long skirt of some old purple damask curtains. Tommy Yelverton wore an old militia coat, a tin helmet, and a large paper-knife for a sword. But all splendours paled before Billy's. A scarlet dressing-gown, a pair of brilliant blue bedroom slippers, an old tin sword, a wreath of artificial flowers, and a glass necklace composed of bits of a crystal chandelier which had once adorned the hall ceiling, were all accommodated on his small person as he arranged the properties for his drama.

The Chinese idol was the most important. It usually held open the tired front door, but was now elevated to a bench and the dignity of the King of England. On its royal head reposed a Crown Derby bowl, chosen for a crown because its pattern was on the outside and, turned upside down, showed most beautifully.

"Now," said Billy, and curtsied. Tommy Yelverton, trying to do likewise, sat down on the fire-irons with the crash of doom.

"Men don't curtsy!" Nan shrieked hastily. "They only bow."

"Saw a picture of some man curtsying to an emperor," Billy returned pugnaciously. "I did."

"Go it!" shouted Tommy Yelverton, sitting down once more among the fire-irons with rapture at the noise.

"Is this Happy Valley?" interposed a clear voice. It was remarkably unexpected, and Nan turned. In the doorway stood a lady—cool, immaculate, in white from her hat to her shoes. If she said anything else it was lost in the voice of Doll, as she rushed to demolish the intruder.

"Come here, Doll," commanded Nan. Something in the horror of the lady's face made her almost prostrate with laughter, as she struggled gallantly to speak. "This is Happy-Valley," she got out at last, advancing with the forgotten feather duster triumphantly bobbing in her hair. "Why?"

But Lil had presence of mind.

"Did you want to see Mrs. Addington?" she inquired.

"I am Mrs. Sinclair," said the apparition, coldly.

"Gee!" said Tommy Yelverton. And Nan whispered softly to Billy:

"Fly, and tell Mother!"

Mrs. Addington would not have been led to say "Gee!" by anything in this mortal life. Yet perhaps what she did say amounted to just that word, as she started bolt upright from her bed.

"Cousin Adelaide—and there's nothing for supper! And Rose—Rose isn't coming till to-morrow!"

CHAPTER II

THE ENGINE

MRS. SINCLAIR sat down on the chair Nan hastily cleared for her, but she shook her head at the offer of tea or lemonade. Cousin Adelaide, Nan thought, didn't seem really friendly. She merely gazed at the extraordinary group before her, and looked thoroughly annoyed.

Billy, breathless, informed her that his mother was coming, and slid over to her, still wearing his glass necklace and looking as pretty as only Billy could. No one who cared for children could have resisted the soft curls of his shining head and his smiling blue eyes. But Mrs. Sinclair gave no sign.

" That idol—we pretended he was the King of England, and we were all courting him," he chuckled, and turned severely as Nan laughed. " Nan said a man would never curtsy, but he would—wouldn't he ? Just bowing is too easy."

" A man would never curtsy ! " Cold and uninterested was the mien of the new cousin.

" I thought you'd know." Billy was undismayed. " And does the Queen of England go to bed in her crown ? "

Stony indifference was the only answer, but no one had ever been indifferent to Billy, who merely thought the new cousin was shy. He grasped the Boarder and set that fluffy white animal on Mrs. Sinclair's knee, with the proud introduction : " My new dog."

Cousin Adelaide shook the Boarder off, though perhaps it was merely that she rose as Mrs. Addington ran down the narrow, mahogany railed stairs.

" I'm so sorry, I really didn't expect you so soon, Adelaide," she said, sweetly. " I should have met you. And where is your luggage ? "

" Coming, I walked here. Are these your children, Mary ? " . Cousin Adelaide glanced at Billy's glass adornments, fixed her eyes on Nan's ridiculous feather duster, still waving gallantly on her head, and finally stared disapprovingly at Lil's trailing satin.

Lil flushed, and tore it off, as she and Nan disappeared at a nod from their mother. There was nothing for supper, and no one to cook, was the thought that choked her. But Billy, the undismayed, trotted off for Rose—the idea was his own—and returned with her clasped firmly by the hand so that she could not escape.

"Now, don't you worry your ma any," said that functionary, as the situation was explained to her. "Just you leave it to me. I see a ham bone can be scraped and done up elegant with eggs, and I'll make a strawberry short-cake like your cousin's never seen."

"Rose! I love you, Rose!" Billy hugged her ecstatically.

"Which—me or the short-cake?" But she gave him a loving pat as Nan flew off to put hot water and clean towels in the guest-room.

Lil's thoughts were elsewhere as she laid the supper table, and slipped out into the garden for roses for it. If Cousin Adelaide were as frosty as this she would be no use in impressing the Yelvertons. Tony would only say—— But Lil shrieked herself: "Oh, my goodness, how you startled me!"

Tony Yelverton stood behind the roses not a yard away, very tall in his tennis flannels and good-looking in a pale, puffy way, with sleek black hair combed back straight from his forehead. "Sorry," he returned rather patronizingly. "I only wanted to know if you'd come sailing with me to-morrow?"

"Mother won't let me." Lil was rattled, or it never would have come out. "Besides, the Allen boys are camping in the Cove, and I'm going over there to a picnic."

"Oh, all right!" said Tony, stiffly, and marched away.

"Bother," Lil gulped, rather blindly. Tony was older than any boy she knew, and all the girls admired him. Now he had gone away offended. "Just because I let out Mother was prejudiced against him," she summed up, crossly. "I wish that horrid Cousin Adelaide wasn't here, and I could have taken time to smooth him down."

Cousin Adelaide, seated in the guest-room, was very near wishing she was not there herself. She had been stunned almost to speechlessness on her arrival at finding Mary Addington in such surroundings. "One living-room, children running wild, everything dreadful," she thought, appalled, pushing away the memory that the children had been strangely attractive. She supposed Mary could only have about two servants, but one of them would have to unstrap her trunks for her. And she rang her bell.

"Did you want anything, Cousin?" Nan appeared in the door, having removed the feather duster from her head.

" You're Nan ? Yes, dear. Will you send one of the servants to undo my trunk ? "

" I'll do it."

" Oh, no, I couldn't think of it ! You might hurt your hands."

" But you see, there aren't any servants," said Nan, cheerfully. " We only have Rose, and she's getting supper in the kitchen. But even she is not here sometimes."

" Do you mean your mother goes without any servants at all ? "

" Mother can't afford them.", Nan never even flushed when she stooped over the refractory strap. " Didn't you know we worked ourselves —all of us ? "

Cousin Adelaide folded her lips tight. Suddenly she bent over her open trunk, and produced a huge bundle. " For Billy," she said, with a smile that made Nan change her mind about the silent, horrified cousin who had descended on her and her feather duster. " I didn't bring any gifts for you and your sister. I wasn't sure what you would like. Perhaps you could give me a hint now on what would be nice for Lil."

Nan said shyly that she thought she could, but the big bundle in her arms was all she really thought of.

"Oh, Billy, it's for you!" she burst out, rushing down to where the little boy sat on the veranda steps. "From Cousin Adelaide. Hurry! I'm just crazy to see what is inside it!"

"P'raps it's a wheelbarrow. Or—oh, Nan, do you think it's a horse and cart?" Billy gasped as Nan cut the string. "It couldn't be an—— Oh, it is, Nanny, it's an aigine— a real, big, red aigine!"

"*Engine*, goose; not aigine," Nan shrieked.

But Billy was beyond words, and already coasting down the garden path on the treasure. Even supper was without power to charm, and Cousin Adelaide smiled as she watched him. She smiled again at supper, as she admired Rose's cooking. The eggs done up with ham were delicious, the biscuits were lighter than beaten white of egg, and the strawberry short-cake called forth the guest's deep admiration. Nan beamed; but Lil was silent.

"It must be so different from all you're used to," she ventured at last.

And Cousin Adelaide rejoined unexpectedly: "Yes. That's the great charm of it!"

Billy, having drunk his milk, had hastened out again. The birds of the air had somehow carried the news of the engine to Tommy

Yelverton, who had arrived panting, to offer
his best knife for it. But Billy, who had
regarded that knife as the most desirable
possession in the whole wide world, refused
with scorn. A common knife for an engine—
an absolutely beautiful scarlet engine on
wheels—was unspeakable. But he hand-
somely allowed Tommy rides on it, and the
two coasted down the path and toiled up with
great ardour.

"What shall I give you, Lil?" asked Cousin
Adelaide, suddenly.

"May I tell you truly?" Lil clasped her
hands to get courage to speak.

"Of course! I asked you."

"Well, it's only—would you come over to
the Yelvertons' with me? They're rich, but
they have no relations like you. And they
despise us——"

"Lil!" said her mother, warningly.

"Was it horrid of me to say it? But it's
true. And they'd know we weren't horrid
common people if they only saw Cousin Adelaide
in that dress. I know it sounds dreadful, but if
you all only *knew*!"

"Of course I'll go, anywhere you like," said
Cousin Adelaide, quietly. "But that's not a
present, Lil, and I want to give you one. Shall

3

it be a dress ? " and as Lil nodded, she laughed and finished, " Yes, a really pretty dress."

" It's perfectly heavenly of her, isn't it, Nan ? " Lil said as they were going to bed. " What do you suppose she'll give you ? "

" Don't know—haven't thought of it. I'd love to see her impressing the Yelvertons for you ; but why on earth do you want her to ? "

" They think money's everything," Lil justified herself hastily. " They talk as if we were only strawberry farmers ! "

" They're common," Nan interjected shrewdly and put out the light. " Do go to sleep, Lil ; you're as bad as Billy about Cousin Adelaide. He's put his engine under his bed, and has Doll and the Boarder guarding it. And for gracious' sake don't go anywhere with Cousin Adelaide to-morrow—we promised to go over to the boys' camp for supper."

" Bother ! " said Lil.

" The boys " were only the Allens and the Marshes—two of each, younger than Lil, and only what she called " dull, all-the-year-round neighbours." There was no excitement to be looked for from the boys. But even Lil's spirits rose as she and Nan rowed across the bay towards the Cove whence the noise of the cheerful campers drifted over the water and the smoke rose up from their fire. Their tents were pitched on a rocky bluff, and their two sail-boats anchored in the deep water under it. Dick Allen scrambled to his feet in one of them as the girls' old green boat drew near.

"What have you brought us?" he shouted. "Just yourselves, or anything to eat?"

"Both," Lil called, indignantly. "Why, the boat's just crowded with baskets. Oh, Nan, look out! You put the sooty kettle on me!"

"You'll wash!" Dick slid perilously into their passing boat. "You've a mighty good-sized supper there. You've saved our lives; all we have left is potatoes."

He shouted for his brother Frank and the two Marsh boys, and hauled out the baskets as the boat touched shore. It was Nan who ordered the kettle filled and more wood put on the fire; Nan who put the potatoes on to bake and the eggs to boil, cut up the corn-cake and made the coffee. A huge basket of strawberries, too small for market, created a vast sensation; but Frank Allen said it was a shame the girls had had to pick them all. They ought to have come over to help, only they had been to a regatta.

"Nan, you and Lil are bricks!" Dick Allen cut in, with conviction. "Here, boys, let's get some more water ! I know Nan will make us wash up."

The feast was spread as the boys returned from the spring, and Nan shrieking as she snatched hot potatoes from the fire. The six were beginning the first course of them, very black and deliciously flavoured with wood ashes, when every hand was arrested with a black and butter-dripping potato halfway to their mouths.

Crash—tear—slide—came from the wooded bank behind them. Then bump ! as someone heavy landed on his feet from the hill above.

" Who on earth's fallen off the roof now ? " said Dick, calmly.

" Oh, don't," Nan gasped. " I can see a man ! I believe—— Dick, you don't think it's *tramps* ? "

" It's somebody who wasn't asked," Dick muttered, staring over his shoulder. " Well, what gall ! "

Tony Yelverton was scrambling out from the bushes.

CHAPTER III

THE PIRATES IN THE COVE

" It's only me," he observed, strolling into the circle. " Hullo, boys, I think you might ask me to join when you give a ladies' party ! "

" It's the girls' party," Dick returned, grimly.

" But of course we'll ask you," said Lil, sweetly. " Come and sit down now."

" You'll have to help wash up ! " Nan had no use for Tony Yelverton, and was pretty sure her mother disliked him.

Dick whispered to her : " Shall I tell him to get out ? You don't want him ! "

" I suppose we can't be so rude "—regretfully. " Make him go and get wood to keep the fire up with, though, before he sits down ! "

But Tony had calmly sat down already. He had tried to move a Marsh boy, each of whom sat one side of Lil, and been ordered to find a seat for himself. Conversation halted under the supercilious eye of the uninvited guest, till he inquired if any of them had been to New York to see the latest musical comedy.

" Of course not, and you know we haven't," returned the Marshes, with one voice.

Nan politely inquired if he wasn't frightfully keen on football. And when she heard he cared more for card-parties and billiards announced with candour that she thought his going to college was a real waste of time. Dick Allen, who was too polite to agree, observed hastily that he was going to college himself after vacation, and wondered if he'd get a chance at football. He captained the High School team, and the Marshes, who went to a rival establishment, grinned placidly that he wouldn't cut enough ice. Nan dashed into the argument at the top of her voice, till dark came down and they sang college songs while they sat around the fire.

" Goodness, we must go ! It's so hard to moor the boat when you can't see, not to mention getting up at five to-morrow to send off the last of the big strawberries," said Nan who never could hold her tongue, though Lil repeatedly warned her that no one took any interest in her affairs.

" We'll moor for you," Dick returned. " You fellows get the dinghy, and we'll see the girls safely over. We'll come back for you, Yelverton, unless you're going to walk round the bay home."

" I've a canoe," said Tony, calmly. " I was going to paddle Lil home in it."

Dick Allen suddenly became stiffly older than his years. " Well, you can't ; Lil's mother wouldn't have it," he observed, crushingly. " And next time you arrive at a picnic you can come from your canoe like a Christian instead of going round the back way. 'Night."

Lil said nothing till they were across the bay and climbing the hill to the house. Then she muttered, stiffly : " I don't see why the boys wouldn't even let Tony come over with us."

" Because he's just a horrid snip," Nan yawned. " Think of going to college, and not being in any games but *cards* ! I wonder who on earth told him where we were. It was just cheek to come and join us when he hadn't been asked."

" I suppose he heard us, and saw the fire," said Lil, slowly, and then despised herself. " If you want to know, I told him yesterday we were going over with the boys."

" Oh, you silly ! We nearly ended the party with a fight," Nan began loftily, and was quenched as she went into the house.

" Nan," Cousin Adelaide gasped at her, " look at yourself. I don't know whether your face or your dress has more black on it ! "

" That was the kettle "—rather ruefully. " Don't look at me, cousin, I always get black. And we had a perfectly elegant time."

" You let them go out alone like this ? " Cousin Adelaide asked, in a puzzled sort of way, as the girls disappeared to put away their baskets.

" Oh, yes ! They're only children, and I like them to enjoy themselves in a childish way as long as they can."

" If I'm not mistaken, Lil won't go on doing so for much longer," Cousin Adelaide commented, rather dryly.

Lil's mother laughed. " I think so. I know all the boys they were with this evening, and they're dear, good boys. Oh, not polished, but they can be trusted ! Oh, Nan ! " she called upstairs, " did you remember to moor the boat ? "

" No," came from Nan. " Dick and the other boys did it when they rowed home with us. We're not coming down again, mother, if you'll excuse us. We're going straight to bed. We have to get up at five."

" Poor children," said Cousin Adelaide, in-

wardly. But her pity was wasted. It was not
five nor even six when Nan awoke, but well on
to seven ; and as she sprang to open the shutters
on the still sleeping Lil she stood paralysed.
What was that in the strawberry garden ?

"Oh, Lil! Oh, mother, mother, come!"
she shrieked, pulling on a frock over her night-
gown. "It's cows."

Cows it was, ten of them, placidly feeding in
the strawberry garden. The plants from which
the day's sale was yet to be picked were all
trampled down, the beds all holes. It meant
dollars and dollars lost. While the Addingtons
slept someone must have broken down a fence
and let the cattle in to feed. Unexpected and
unutterable loss made the three bereft ones
clasp one another's hands in dead silence, till
Nan gasped furiously :

"I'll go and drive them out, or they'll get
into the corn, and eat it all up too. Hurry,
Lil ; get your shoes on, and come and help
me!"

But never were cows so refractory as the ten
the girls hunted that morning. They doubled
and twisted and galloped, anywhere but out
of the earthly paradise in which they had
found themselves. It was after seven before
they were off the premises, and Wood, the old

man-of-all-work, appeared to begin his chores by putting up the broken bit of fence round the ruined garden.

Lil flopped down on the steps beside her sister. " No strawberry picking *this* morning," she said, incautiously.

" You've got your wish." Nan was tired, sad, and thoroughly upset, and she snapped: " You were always saying you hated doing it."

" I'm awfully sorry, Nan, dear ; truly I am ! I never meant it that way."

Lil turned remorsefully, but Nan paid no attention. She felt sick at heart and wanted to cry. Even losing one day's market meant losing money they needed sorely. There was winter coal to buy, besides warm clothes, and Rose certainly ought to be kept on all winter to save their mother, who was looking worried fagged, and weary. And as she reached that doleful place in her reverie, something touched her hand. It was Lil, bearing a brimming cup of tea.

" Cousin Adelaide made it for us, and wasn't it good of her ?   She isn't even up yet, but she has the sweetest little tea basket and spirit kettle beside her bed. Do drink it, Nan."

Nan rubbed her head against her sister's arm.

It was a wordless regret for crossness, but Lil understood.

"Oh, Nan, Billy's in Cousin's room," she added, hastily, "doing a roaring lion under her bed. She says she doesn't mind, but don't you think you could catch him and bring him away? He won't mind me."

"I was so——" Nan gulped her tea, and felt better. "Oh, Lil, such a nasty, evil temper got into me!"

Lil gave her a little squeeze. "I know. Never mind. Hadn't you better get Billy quick? Rose says breakfast is almost ready."

A sudden shriek from the kitchen cut the words off her tongue, and Nan all but dropped Cousin Adelaide's Spode cup.

"Good gracious! can there be more cows? It sounds as if it were tigers," she gasped, and rushed for the kitchen, with Lil at her heels.

"Well, I never! If that don't beat it! What'll your ma say?" Rose flung at them in a volley. "Without a word of a lie, I never saw the like. There's been fairies round!"

"There's been what?" Nan cried. "Oh, Rose, get it out, can't you?"

"It's outside," retorted Rose, more coherently, "and it nearly killed me. Just you go and look!"

"Oh, don't!" gasped Lil. "Rose, is it a drunken man?"

But there was no one where Nan was staring with eyes as big as a saucer. In the yard, by the kitchen window, stood big baskets, little baskets, tin pails, and buckets, all full of their best strawberries—the big, luscious berries that were the last for that year.

"Then the cows"—Nan stood bewildered—"the cows didn't eat them!"

"Cows ain't picked them," Rose retorted, "that's certain."

"I believe Tony Yelverton——" Lil began, and Nan cut her off.

"Not a bit of him! It must have been Wood."

"Wood never gets here a single minute sooner than he need," Rose said, scornfully. "These was picked before sun-up. Oh, look, here's a note!"

Very badly scribbled on a somewhat grubby envelope was this:

> "We picked the berries so
> you wouldn't have to.
>   (Signed)
>   THE PIRATES IN THE COVE."

Under it one of them had drawn a most

realistic skull and cross-bones, which was promptly annexed by Billy, arriving breathless in pink pyjamas.

"Those boys!" Nan shouted. "Well, of all the nice surprises—though we did have an awful shock first!"

"Let's tell mother quick—she's been so worried," Lil exclaimed. And Nan was generous enough not to jeer at her for suggesting Tony Yelverton could have saved the crop, though she chuckled at the thought of Tony out in the damp dawn picking strawberries.

There was plenty to do still: the berries had to be put in their little boxes and the crates filled for market. Cousin Adelaide, to her own astonishment, rather resented not being allowed to labour too. To her great surprise, the Addingtons' simple life had a charm that gripped her. She smiled to herself after a most excellent luncheon of Rose's own omelette, and produced a long bundle that had lain hidden in her lap.

"Lil's parcel," she announced.

But, oh, what a parcel! A piece of thickest, softest *crêpe de Chine* for a dress, and soft white satin for an underslip. Lil gasped with happiness as she opened it, and Nan was almost as pleased.

"Oh, Lil," she burst out, "now you can go to Nettie Yelverton's party!"

"A party?" cried Cousin Adelaide. "Then hadn't we better see about having it made at once? Lil and I should go to the dressmaker's this afternoon."

"Dressmakers charges a nawful lot-er-money," Billy suddenly proclaimed from the background.

"Lot of money isn't one word," Lil said; but her face fell. The small household exchequer could never afford the expense of making up this perfectly beautiful dress.

"The making is my affair," Cousin Adelaide cut in hastily, to lift the cloud that oppressed her kinfolk. "Shall we go now, Lil?"

Lil's conscience tugged hard and stopped her "yes." She had fifty things to do: a shirt-waist to be ironed; and her best cotton wanted pressing.

"I'll do your dress," observed her mother with what the girls called her thought-reading voice.

"No, mummy, thank you ever so much." Lil kissed her. "If Cousin won't mind waiting an hour I can get it all done."

Cousin assented hastily, and realized that in the simple life all unexpected proposals were blocked by the brick wall of fact.

" And perhaps," Lil went on, rather timidly,
" you'd come with me to the Yelvertons' afterwards. You see, they've never seen anyone
connected with an earl——"

" Good heavens ! " said Cousin Adelaide,
rather faintly. " But, yes, of course I'll
come."

" And will you wear your embroidered white
dress ? "

" Oh, do ! " said Nan, rapturously. " They'd
be *impressed* ! "

" You won't like them very much, Adelaide,"
Mrs. Addington warned her.

" Oh, mother, *I* like them," Lil protested.

" You'll get over that," said her mother
cheerfully, and to her astonishment Nan returned under her breath, " I wonder ! "

Nan sprawled comfortably on the steps as
Cousin Adelaide and Lil departed, but not even
to her mother did she explain why Lil really
liked the Yelvertons. Lil was growing up, and
poor, and the rich Yelvertons, with automobiles
and a wonderful house, were her ideals, for the
moment. Tony told her she was pretty, Nettie
let her try on a five-thousand-dollar pearl
necklace, Mr. Yelverton supplied her with five-
pound boxes of expensive candy ; and there
was no use in saying a derogatory word about

any of them, unless Cousin Adelaide—— Nan
sat up with a sudden chuckle.

" Mother," she inquired, abruptly, " do you
think Cousin Adelaide will be as stiff as she
can be to the Yelvertons, or only about half as
stiff ?—because her point of view of them is
about the only òne that can affect Lil's."

CHAPTER IV

LIL'S NEW DRESS

BUT for once Lil had forgotten even the Yelvertons.

Her visit to the dressmaker was a glimpse of Fairyland. Cousin Adelaide knew more of the fashions than even the great Miss Hunt, whose creations the Addingtons had heard of but had never been able to afford. It was a blissful hour spent while being fitted with a brown holland pattern and talked of as a personality. Lil felt grown-up at last, as Miss Hunt proclaimed with ardour that Cousin Adelaide's ideas were most Parisian, and so suitable for a young lady, " who was just coming out ! "

" I've never half thanked you," Lil said, clutching Cousin Adelaide as they left Miss Hunt's enthralling rooms. " Oh, I don't even know how to begin ! "

" You've said more than you know." Cousin Adelaide laughed. " You will look very nice, my dear, in that little dress."

" Little dress ! " Lil gasped. This marvellous
garment was only a little dress ! " Cousin
Adelaide, it's a—dream ! "

Cousin Adelaide nodded carelessly. " You're
very like your father, Lil ; you have his looks.
He was most lovable, too. I was very fond
of him."

Lil remembered him quite well, but she had
never thought of his looks. She said " Oh ! "
rather vaguely, and came out with the real
thing in her head : " Cousin Adelaide, why
didn't you let Miss Hunt cut my dress really
low for the party ? "

" Because the little V-neck was far more
suitable and becoming. You're not out yet,
you know." Cousin Adelaide was a little
thrown back on herself.

" But I never shall come out like other
girls." Lil had longed to show her pretty
shoulders, that were so much whiter than
Nettie Yelverton's. " I shall always have to
toil in our old strawberry garden."

" Well, it's a happy life, for just now." And
it was, since the whole year could not be spent
in picking strawberries. " Fortunately, you see,
you're young."

" That makes it worse."

" Not when you've everything to look forward to," and Cousin Adelaide calmly changed the subject. " What would Nan like for a present, Lil ? I must get her something."

Lil pondered.

" Nan doesn't care much about clothes, but, all the same, I think she ought to join the dress-making class next winter. You can see it would be a help for Mother if Nan would only take an interest in it."

" That's a good idea "—thoughtfully. " She could learn and Nan's going to be very difficult to dress. She will be such a beauty that she'll need to understand herself."

" What ? " Lil stopped dead in the middle of the road to the Yelvertons', paralysed with amazement. " *Nan* a beauty ! Why, she's awkward, and her hair's never tidy, and her eyes are almost green ! "

" There's an old story about an ugly duckling——"

But Lil shook her head. " Oh, Cousin, don't ! I love Nan, but I can't think she could ever be considered pretty."

" Not pretty," Cousin Adelaide corrected coolly. " I said Nan would be more than pretty. Those green eyes are as changeable as the sea, and that untidy hair curls, even out in the rain. She has expression and personality, and that greatest gift of charm. In three or four years, perhaps longer, for she'll grow up slowly, Nan will create a sensation, wherever she is! I hope I may see it."

"Oh!" said Lil incredulously, and nearly walked on past the Yelvertons' gate. "We turn in here, Cousin Adelaide. This is the avenue."

"What does Mr. Yelverton do?" Cousin Adelaide asked, suddenly, as they came in sight of the Yelvertons' yellow marble house, with its seven kinds of windows.

"He makes money," Lil returned, succinctly. "Oh, Cousin Adelaide, do like them!"

But Cousin Adelaide was doing something else as she sat down in a raspberry-coloured drawing-room on a gilded chair. Even as she was introduced to Mrs. Yelverton and her daughter she realized why Lil's mother was reluctant to let her see much of them. Both were dressed for a garden-party, and a joke of Nan's that Nettie Yelverton had twelve new *crêpe de Chine* dresses, and looked as if she wore them all at once, recurred to Nan's cousin.

But there was no doubt about their welcome. Mrs. Yelverton planned at once to ask the Addingtons' cousin to stay with them. Even if she refused, the name of the Honorable Mrs.

Sinclair could head the list of invited guests at a week-end house-party. She had almost said so, as she ladled out the rum punch which replaced tea in the Yelverton house, and Nettie and Tony Yelverton seized upon Lil, to giggle with in a corner of the red and gold drawing-room.

" You liked them, didn't you ? " Lil asked, as Cousin Adelaide was strolling home in silence.

" I think they mean well," cautiously. Only pure dismay had made Cousin Adelaide gracious, as her hostess told her the cost of every article in her glaring drawing-room.

" But you can't say Nettie isn't pretty ? "

" Well—yes." Cousin Adelaide grudged having to agree. " But, my dear, model yourself and your style on your mother—the most perfect gentlewoman I have ever met." She could hardly explain how much she admired Mrs. Addington for her want of self-consciousness, for the simple way she had entertained her just as a humble purse could provide ; all that could not be said to Lil, and yet how good it might have been for the girl to hear it !

But Lil was listening to nothing. " Tony Yelverton thinks my new dress will be lovely ! "

she exclaimed, " and I've promised him five dances at Nettie's party."

" Tony seems a very ill-bred boy." Cousin Adelaide waked up suddenly. " His manners are appalling. When you know more of nice young men you will not attach any importance to the opinions of Tony Yelverton." After this bombshell Cousin Adelaide relapsed into silence, till she found herself being welcomed by Billy on the Addingtons' cool veranda.

" The sun's very hot, Billy," she said, as she sank into a chair and Lil disappeared in search of her mother.

Billy was never at a loss for conversation. " When I was little I used to think it was like a candle, and Mother could blow it out," he returned. " Doll and the Boarder look nice, cousin, don't they ? I've just washed them.

" Very." Cousin Adelaide glanced politely at the very black Doll and the very white Boarder, seated affably at her feet. " I suppose you won't be keeping the Boarder for very much longer ? "

" I'm keeping him for ever "—calmly. " Cousin, have you seen Mr. Bowser ? "

" Who is Mr. Bowser ? "

" My stuffed animal with a squeak in his tail when you pull it. Wait, I'll tell the dog family

to get him! Doll and Boarder "—sharply—
" where is Mr. Bowser ? "

The dog family disappeared into the house
with a wild rush.

" Now they'll shriek," said the proud pro-
prietor. " They hate Mr. Bowser because he's
a cat, or he might be a rabbit. You wait."

But dead silence reigned in the house. Billy
creeping after his dogs to see why, suddenly
turned and waved frantically.

" Come quick, cousin ! Oh, do ! Get down
on your hands and knees and creep, or they'll
see you."

Nothing in Cousin Adelaide's career had
astonished her so much as to find herself
obediently crawling along the floor in her best
white embroidered dress; but there was something magnetic about Billy.   Inside the hall she
saw the cat, or " it might have been a rabbit,"
its head held by Doll and its tail by the Boarder.
Suddenly, and sure enough, it squeaked !

The dogs stood still in amazement.   Then the
Boarder gently pulled the tail of Mr. Bowser
again, and Billy's chuckle burst out of him.
Cousin Adelaide found herself laughing con-
tagiously, or did Billy Boy really make her feel
younger and gayer ?

" Mr. Bowser may be tired," he announced,

bouncing into the fray and seizing the trophy from its enraptured captors. But it was the stately Cousin Adelaide who put it safely on the high shelf by the clock, and returned of her own accord to Billy's society on the veranda. " I think the Boarder should have a more stay-for-ever name," he observed. "Don't you, cousin ? "

" Is Mr. Bowser a rabbit or a cat ? " demanded Cousin Adelaide.

" Cat "—firmly.

" Then why don't you change *his* name? There is a lovely cat called ' Hidigeigei ' in a German book."

" Oh, but that name would do for the Boarder! It's so *important*."

" But it's a cat's name."

" Boarder wouldn't ever know that, and I like it." Billy rushed off to impress on the Boarder that his name was changed to Hidigeigei, as Nan brought her sewing and sat down by Cousin Adelaide.

" I wish we had something nice to do to-morrow," she observed, and Mrs. Addington, who had come out to gather in Billy, turned suddenly.

" Why, you have, Nan," she said, " only I forgot to tell you. You are going sailing with

Dick and Frank Allen.   They came this afternoon to ask you.

"What ?   But I never saw them ! "

"You were picking peas, and Dick wouldn't
wait.   He was afraid "—smiling—" of being
thanked for gathering the strawberries."

But Nan cast down her sewing with a wail.
"Mother, I can't go !   To-morrow will be my
last violin lesson.   Oh, mummy, say I may
miss it ?   You know I'm no good, and I'll
never play ; and Herr Schneider despises my
efforts."

"He told me you had no talent for it,
certainly"—with rather a rueful smile.   "I'll
see, Nan.   But I think you can go with the
boys."

Nan slipped off to find Lil.   Billy, totally
forgotten when he sat with a picture book,
under orders to "cool off," was suddenly over-
come with horror.   Cousin Adelaide was saying
for Nan to go sailing and break into her violin
hour, even if it was her last lesson.   Sailing was
the one thing Nan loved, and Cousin Adelaide
wanted her to stay at home just because that
old German man was coming !

"Nan is such a tomboy," Cousin Adelaide
said slowly.   "You let her run too wild,
Mary."

"I ran wild when I was a girl," Mrs. Addington retorted.

"Oh, you—yes. But Nan is somehow different."

Mrs. Addington shook her head. Billy, with his eyes on his book, never saw it, and thought she had not answered Cousin. Deep down in his little boy's mind he feared, horribly, that Nan was going to be disappointed. And Billy did love Nan.

As she put him to bed that night he hugged her hard.

"I want you to go sailing, Nannie."

"Yes, dear, I'm going, unless Herr Schneider comes before I get off. Would you like to come too, Billy? I know the boys wouldn't mind, if mother's willing."

"No, thank you, I must stay at home," Billy returned politely. "I have—have 'portant business to attend to."

Nan smiled and tucked him in, asked for the Boarder's health, and was told to speak of Hidigeigei, not Boarder. But as she went off to her own room Bill was thoughtful for the one minute and a half that elapsed before he fell asleep.

CHAPTER V

BILLY THE JAILER

ROSE was cross.

She had a toothache and knew the offending member should come out, but she did not want to go to the dentist. It was baking day, and she had all the bread on her hands, besides some ironing that had been neglected the day before. She bounced a beefsteak pie from the oven to the kitchen table, and glanced at a noble lemon layer-cake that lay beside it, all ready for the midday dinner.

" And can't eat a bite of it, for this plaguey tooth," she muttered, sourly, as she turned and plunged her hands into the half-made bread.

It was no propitious moment for Nan to burst into the kitchen with a demand for food to take out sailing with the boys. Rose refused bluntly to give her any, with the rider that she didn't hold with picnics, and Miss Lil would get all tired out.

59

" Well ! " said Nan, indignantly. She glanced at the unpleasant back Rose turned on her, made a flying swoop on the kitchen table, and was gone, with Rose's meat pie in one hand and her layer-cake in the other.

" Give 'em back this minute ! " Rose shrieked after her. " You can't have 'em ! You——" But Nan was out of range, flying down the garden path with the family dinner. " My land ! " said Rose weakly. She sat down in the nearest chair and laughed, with a sudden hand clapped to her cheek. Her plunge after Nan had broken the gumboil that was the cause of all her pain ! She was rather grateful to Nan, in spite of the lost dinner, as she " bounced up " a dish of hot biscuits and heated some cold chicken.

Nan had no thought of Rose as she bore her heavy loot down to the shore, where stood an immaculate Lil in blue cotton and a shady hat.

" Well," said Lil, despairingly, " you're a sight ! " The gravy of the stolen pie had run down the front of Nan's skirt, her unruly hair was on end, her hat hung down her back. That hat was a bone of contention between the two in any case : it had cost five cents, and was trimmed with red muslin and strings to tie under

Nan's chin. No other such hat had ever been
seen, and Nan adored it. Lil detested it
frankly. " That hat," she groaned, " and—
oh, stand still, Nan, till I get some of the gravy
off. You're dreadful ! "

" Oh, never mind—we can't both look nice,
and you're just like the girl on the outside of
a Summer Number ! But you haven't been
plundering the larder and circumventing Rose ;
if we both looked handsome we'd probably
have had to starve. Now I've offended Rose,
stolen the family's dinner, and spoilt my
appearance—but anyway we'll not go hungry,
and I've got off before Herr Schneider could
roll up "—with satisfaction. " Here's the yacht !
Hop into the boat and help me pull her out to
the buoy, so that the boys can take us off in
deep water."

The fastidious Lil glanced from her clean dress
to the wet rope ; but she pulled energetically
when she did pull. The boys tacked over to
them on a short leg, came about just by the
boat, and as the yacht was at its nearest Lil
jumped on board. Nan handed over her plunder
and made a flying leap after it, fell short as the
yacht gathered way, and landed with one foot
square on the lemon layer-cake.

Loud cheers greeted this exploit, with jeers

from the boys that Nan had done it on purpose
to be able to eat most of the cake herself.

"Want to steer, Nan," Dick Allen asked,
as he helped Lil to the best seat and provided
her with a cushion. The boys admired Lil
immensely, but Nan was just one of themselves ;
she never needed help, and they would no
more have offered her a cushion than they
would to another boy.

Nan took the tiller. Dick Allen sat with the
sheet in his hand, and the Marsh boys lay
ready by the jib, for the wind was against the
old " Phantom," which had once been a smart
two-ton cutter, and they had to tack till they
rounded the point of the bay. Frank Allen
produced a pocketful of green apples, which
were accepted by all the crew, though they
were far too youthful.

> " ' Johnny Jones and his Sister Sue,
> Bit a peach of an emerald hue,' "

said Nan, throwing hers overboard. " Boys,
your apples are awful—but they're better than
having to sit at home with Herr Schneider ! "

She was not troubled as to what had made
that punctual gentleman so late, but Billy
might have told her. He had withdrawn after
breakfast to a seat by the front gate, full of

alarm lest his Nannie might miss her sail—
which was the " 'portant business " he had
mentioned to her. If Herr Schneider arrived
before Nan started, Billy was sure Cousin
Adelaide's counsels would prevail, and his
mother keep poor Nan at home.

" I'm awful 'fraid of him," he thought,
gloomily. " But, oh, here he is," as a small
and stout gentleman appeared up the road.
" There isn't any lesson," Billy blurted, fiercely.
" My Nannie has gone out—out for the day ! "

Herr Schneider stopped by the gate.

" Ach, no, little boy ! " he returned, scornfully. " She waits for her last lesson."

" She can't have a lesson, because she has
gone off in a boat—a ship." Billy was in-
furiated.

But Herr Schneider was dense. " She waits
to have her last lesson," said he.

Billy gazed at him, desperate. Nannie might
have gone (and she might not), and Cousin
Adelaide—" Well, come along then, and look
for her," said the trembling Billy. " Come,
Hidigeigei," to the ever-present Boarder.

" Why do you call a dog Hidigeigei ? It is
a cat's name," panted Herr Schneider instruc-
tively. " A most lovely, ever-to-be-admired
cat."

It was the last straw. " It's a dog's name now," said Billy, and turned Herr Schneider sharply along the path which led past the back of the house to the stable. " In here," he commanded, pulling open the door of the harness-room.

" In, you say, little boy ? " Herr Schneider wiped his brow. " Ach, Miss Nan is here, no doubt ! Is it not so ? "

Billy banged the door on him for sole answer, bolted it, and sat down outside to wait. It would not be long—as soon as he saw the " Phantom's " sails out in the bay he would know Nan was safely on board and let Herr Schneider out. But at an unexpected, joyful yell behind him he turned his head.

" Billy ! " Tommy Yelverton's voice was the voice of joyful frenzy. " Say, I've got a new boat ! It goes by steam ; come on down to the duckpond and try it."

" I'll be back in a minute," Billy yelled casually to the unseen Herr Schneider and was off like a streak. And the wretched Herr Schneider sat down on a hard chair in the harness-room, a somewhat dark apartment with no window, waiting for his pupil, whom that so strange little boy had probably gone to bring.

It was half an hour afterwards when Cousin
Adelaide suddenly appeared on the veranda.

" Someone," said she, " is howling. Can it
be one of Billy's dogs ? Could they have got
hurt ? "

Mrs. Addington looked up from her mending.
" It's more probably Billy and Tommy Yelverton
being Indians," she said, carelessly.

" No, listen." Cousin Adelaide stood rigid.
" It's somebody in trouble."

Far away and muffled there rose appalling
yells, then bangs ; then more yells, mixed with
strange exclamations.

" It sounds like a lunatic." Cousin Adelaide
was pale.

" It sounds like Herr Schneider—only I sent
Wood into the village in the wagon to stop him
coming," gasped Mrs. Addington. " Has Wood
come back ? "

But a fearful howl brought her to her feet,
and sent her flying towards the noise, and the
stable.

" It's someone being killed," cried Cousin
Adelaide, trailing after her. But a panting,
red-faced Billy brought both ladies up short.

" I'm 'fraid—'fraid to let him out." He
danced round his mother in anguish. " He's
making such a noise in there. Oh, mummy,

5

don't go near! He'll kill you! I'm 'fraid
he's turned into something else from Herr
Schneider.   I only just locked him in and forgot
him."

"Where is he?" his mother demanded.

"In the harness-room—and there's a chair,
mother."

"Why, Billy Addington, what have you been
doing?"

But Mrs. Addington's words were drowned
in a torrent of wails and yelps from the prisoner.
Awful German words she fortunately did not
understand were hurled at her as she un-
fastened the bolted door, and with the speed
of a rifle bullet Herr Schneider shot forth,
gesticulating and grasping a stick. His head
down, he all but knocked over Cousin Adelaide,
who stood an amazed spectator, and butted
into old Wood, who had just arrived and
descended from his empty wagon.

"I will give you any dollars you like, man,"
roared Her Schneider, "to drive me away from
this place of crazies!"   He climbed wildly
into Wood's wagon, and collapsed in a hunched-
up heap on its floor.

"What *is* the matter?" Mrs. Addington
tried hopelessly to get at the sense of it all.
"Herr Schneider, what happened to you?   I

sent Wood in to tell you not to come to-day—
that my daughter would not have a lesson.
I never dreamed you had got here."

But Herr Schneider would not be pacified.
" No, no, you did not send," he roared. " I
walk out, and the little boy, he lock me in. He
is a most bad, a most abominable little boy ! "

" You're crazy," burst in Wood, who adored
Billy. " You get out of my wagon ! "

" Oh, just wait, Wood ! " Mrs. Addington
laid a hand on Herr Schneider's arm. " Won't
you listen to me ? " she pleaded. " It is all a
mistake—a dreadful mistake. Please come to
the house and let me explain it to you—you
really must, Herr Schneider."

Schneider got out of the wagon, and looked
furiously about him, but Mrs. Addington's
gentle voice had appeased him, none the less.

" I feel as if I had been in an asylum—the
one where you put the people who have no
sense ! " he exclaimed, and Mrs. Addington
turned to Billy.

" Oh, Billy, why did you lock this poor
gentleman in ? " she demanded. " What did
you mean, dear ? "

" Cousin Adelaide said "—tears smudged
Billy's crimson face—" she said Nan ought to
stay for her lesson, and he did come before

Nan started. That's why I locked him in the
harness-room. And I forgot him. Oh, don't
be cross! I meant to let him out quick, but we
went to sail Tommy's new boat, and I forgot
him!"

"But, Billy, dear, it was dreadfully wrong
to lock him in at all."

"You can't feel more worse than I do,"
gasped Billy. Mummy understood why he had
done it. Mummy always understood—but
Cousin Adelaide's cold gaze made him shiver.

"Of course, Billy will apologize to Herr
Schneider at once," she remarked, stiffly, and
swept Herr Schneider off to the veranda, where
curiously enough, he soon found himself
sufficiently appeased to accept a cup of coffee
and to talk to Cousin Adelaide, whom he
announced to be an exceptionally cultivated
lady.

Billy went bravely up to the pair and begged
the poor victim's pardon most humbly. Much
mollified, Herr Schneider arose, made low bows
to the ladies, and departed.

Cousin Adelaide gazed after him, being what
Nan called "as stiff as she could be."

"Really, Mary," she said to Mrs. Addington,
in her coldest voice, "I can't consider it was all
a misfortune to lose Herr Schneider's tuition.

His language—in the harness-room, and coming out of it—was not that of a preceptor of girls. I——" she stooped suddenly, swooped Billy into her arms, and kissed him. " Oh, Mary !" she said, helplessly, and began to laugh like a girl.

CHAPTER VI

OUTSIDE THE BIG SHOAL

THERE were two ways to round the point that
cut Happy Valley Bay off from the open sea.
One—despised and safe—through a narrow
passage inside the long, black shoal that ran out
half a mile in low water ; the other outside it,
through open water. It was outside the shoal
that Nan steered the Phantom, and hung her
up in the light breeze while the crew lunched.
When the tide was high the shoal could be
hugged close ; when it was low even the small
Phantom had to give the rocks a wide berth.
Nan laid the boat to in a betwixt and between
sort of place, but the crew of the Phantom
was not particularly considering such things,
being occupied with the more absorbing subject
of food.

The boys had all brought something, from
cold meat to chocolate. Nan's provender was
considered splendid, especially the footprint in
the layer-cake, which was carefully served to

her, as the biggest part. The afternoon breeze had died to a dead calm, and after-lunch laziness descended on even the Marsh boys, when Lil looked round idly.

" We've drifted in an awful lot," she yawned. " Why didn't you boys put an ancher down ? Look, the water's shallow as shallow ! "

" What ? " Dick Allen jumped to his feet, cast a glance behind him, and whistled. The shoal was under them, not behind them, and not even a breath of wind ruffled the wide bay. " Get the sweeps out, boys," he commanded. " Get some way on her ! "

Nan hung over the Phantom's bows, as the useless sails flapped idly, and the boys flung out the big oars and began to pull.

"Back," she yelled. "Back water! Quick!" And fell over the cockpit with the Phantom's furious bump. There was a curious settling feeling as the yacht brought up dead still.

" Taken ground," said Dick Allen, coolly. " Try piling into the stern ! "

Piling into the stern and jumping was useless. The boys swarmed overboard and tried to shove the bow off, and might as well have tried to shift a house. Nothing would move the Phantom. She was aground, hard and fast on the big shoal, with the tide going out.

They all knew what that meant : no getting
back till midnight, and everybody's mother
waiting on the shore, at the best. Dick and
Frank Allen held a hurried consultation in
whispers. The look of the weather was not
good, and if the sea got up with the rising tide
they might find themselves hard put to it to
keep the Phantom from pounding to pieces.
Both ways the boys knew they ought to get out
of that, and quick.

" The girls can't wait here hours till the next
tide," Dick summed up. " I'd better swim
across the shoal to the village, and get a boat
to take them ashore."

" Nonsense ! " Nan protested. " We can stay
till the tide turns."

" That'll be hours. What do you suppose
your mother would say if you never turned up
till midnight ? No ! You've got to be landed."

" Oh, I wish we hadn't come ! " Lil turned
pale.

" Oh, no, you don't, Lil ; you only imagine
that," Frank Allen cut in, cheerfully. " Dick,
you and Percy Marsh can swim across the shoal
and the inside passage to shore. It isn't far."

But it seemed miles, that took hours, to
the waiting little company marooned on the
Phantom before they saw the boys land on

the opposite point. Nan found a spirit lamp and made some tea they were glad to get, for the sun had vanished in thick clouds, and the rising sea-wind was chill. She insisted on all four eating and drinking, and Frank Allen made a shelter with a spare sail. But even huddled in the cockpit the boy could not hide his apprehension from Nan.

" Don't you get panicky," said she, calmly. " The sea hasn't got up yet."

" It's a horrid looking evening, Nan, but "— he laughed—" I was only worrying about you two girls. You see, if anything happened, we two boys could swim."

" So can I "—promptly, but her face fell. " Lil can't, though."

" That's what's bothering me. For goodness' sake, Nan, how long is it since they went? They ought to be back, unless they can't find a boat."

" Of course they'll find a boat." Nan glanced at the ancient cockpit clock. " They've been gone two hours, if that old thing's right; but they'd have to go up to the fishing village in the Cove for a boat, and that's over a mile along the shore."

" I know "; but he moved, and leaned staring across the shoal.

Lil had stopped trying to talk to the youngest Marsh boy, as being too young to bother about. She put her head down on a coil of rope, since nothing better offered, and went placidly to sleep.

"Wake her," said Frank Allen, sharply. "By George, Nan, here comes the wind, and—we've made a mistake about the tide I It was low at four, and it's turned. Look at the tide-race I "

Nan looked. Far, far out in the leaden bay was a streak of white water, but she had no need to wake Lil. A furious sea-squall struck the Phantom and sent the sail-shelter flying, and Lil bolt upright, staring at the other three.

"We'll never get off now," she gasped. "Frank, the sea's getting up—look at it I And I hear the swell breaking away outside I "

If it was no news it was unpleasantly true. From far off came the steady boom of the long Atlantic rollers, as the boys and girls looked at each other in silence. One and all knew that as the tide rose the water over the shoal would become a mass of boiling breakers, and the finish of the gay little Phantom —unless Dick and Percy Marsh got back with a boat in time I For the present they were safe enough, but——

" I thought I heard a boat." Nan broke the pause, trenchantly. " Listen! "

" So did I." But over the bare rocks of the shoal towards shore they could see nothing. Frank Allen was silent as abruptly as he had spoken, and Lil began to cry.

"Nothing's coming," she sobbed. "Nothing's going to come! We'll all just have to be drowned! "

" Stop crying," said Nan, fiercely. "Listen!"

And from close by, behind the nearest rock, someone shouted : " Phantom, ahoy! "

" It's Dick," said Nan, wildly. " I knew he'd get back. It's—why, it's Tony Yelverton! "

For out from among the maze of rocks, varnished, rowlocked, elegant, came Tony Yelverton's yellow dinghy, instead of the clumsy fisherman's boat with thole-pinned oars.

" Well," said Nan, with a long breath, " I take back every single thing I ever said about him. Fancy *Tony* coming out here! "

" I said you were all perfectly horrid about him! " Lil tore to the lee gunwale. " Oh, Tony, how splendid of you! "

Tony, rather hot and puffy, hauled his dinghy alongside. " I came for the girls," he said, rather pompously. " I met Dick and Percy, but they've gone on to the village for another boat. They wanted to come with me, but I' hadn't room."

" Why not ? " Nan stared at the dinghy's empty stern sheets.

" Because I wasn't going to row those two lumps out here ! Why should I ? "

" Oh, get in, girls, and stop talking." Frank Allen pushed both girls to the lee combings. " Get off as quick as you can with them, Yelverton, and you'd better take young Marsh too. I'm all right here till the other chaps come, but he's got a throat and his mother will be having fits about him. Hop in, George ! "

" Not much, George won't," retorted Mr. Yelverton, with succinct inelegance. " I didn't come out for any fool kids. All I'll take's the girls."

" What ? " Nan drew up her feet where they dangled into his dinghy, as she sat on the Phantom's combing. " Tony Yelverton, you won't get any girls, with that Marsh boy left out here in the sea to get some kind of 'gitis ! Don't you put a foot in his boat, Lil ; don't dare to ! "

" Don't be so silly," Frank exhorted, sharply. " I'll look after Marsh. You two get away with Yelverton. Look out there, and be quick ! "

He sprang from the cockpit on to the taffrail to stare out to sea, and Lil screamed.

" Oh, Nan, it's the first big wave—I felt it
hit us ! Oh, let's get into the boat quick, and
go with Tony. Quick, I felt the yacht *jolt* ! "

" I wouldn't go with such a person," gasped
Nan, and a second jolt flung Lil up against her.

" You needn't." Frank flung himself into
the cockpit between them. " That's the tide ;
there's water under us ! Here, Yelverton, make
yourself useful "—he grabbed a coil of rope and
flung it to Tony. " Make your end fast to your
thwart, and get your boat out forrard of us.
Then pull—pull as hard as you can. Keep your
stern straight. Couple more lifts, and I believe
we'll slither over ! "

" Pull yourself," said Tony Yelverton. " I'm
not going to break my back for your scrap-heap
boat ! She'll sit here all right."

But he choked on the end of it, flat on his
back in the dinghy, with Frank Allen and the
Marsh boy landed on him, making fast his end
of the rope. Even Tony Yelverton had sense
to lie still as each of them took an oar, and put
their back into it.

" Push, girls ; get a sweep and push," Frank
yelled back to them. " I believe I felt her
give. Push ! "

" He's right," cried Nan, electrically. " I
think the water's deep enough to float us

off the shoal point, and straight ahead of us there's lots—if we can only get to it."

But Lil's weight was on the sweep already, and she shook her head. " She's not stirring ; she——"

" Push ! " shrieked Nan. " Frank, she's sliding a little ! I felt her. Oh, Frank ! " Violently, abruptly, the Phantom slithered, lifted to a wave, and swung off the shoal. Nan ran to get up the jib as she glided into deep, breakerless water, and Frank let the dinghy fall back alongside.

" You girls did it," he gasped, as he and the small Marsh boy piled into the yacht and hoisted breathlessly at the mainsail. " Hang on to the tiller, Nan ; don't let her get too much way on. We've got to take Yelverton on board."

" Serve him right if we towed him home like he is, and let him get soaked." Nan glanced at Tony, towing alongside in the smother, by the rope that was still fast to the Phantom's bow.

" No reason we should be hateful, if he was." Frank was wholesomely masculine. " We're clear enough now, Nan. Let me at the tiller and I'll luff up and get him on board."

Tony, extremely wet and correspondingly sulky, dropped down by Nan in the cockpit,

as young Marsh ran aft with the rope to let his
dinghy go astern.

"We don't want you," Nan greeted him,
belligerently. "It was only Frank who let you
get out of your boat, and it's not your fault
that we're off the shoal!"

"It was Tony's boat got us off, anyhow."
Lil defended him indignantly. "Do be sensible, Nan!"

Tony grinned and turned to her. "Say, Lil,
your small sister looks well when she's angry,"
he observed. "This kind of thing suits her too.
Look at her hair, and her eyes—did you see
how they flashed when she hit out at me?
She's going to be a crackajack beauty one
day!"

Lil winced. He had no grateful word for her
championship, only praise for Nan, who had
not been pleasant. She remembered what
Cousin Adelaide had said about Nan's looks, and
it must be true if Tony had noticed them. In
spite of herself Lil gazed at her sister with a
little jealous prick in her heart. Nan had
taken off the five-cent hat that the boys had
laughed at all day, and the wind had ruffled her
hair into a mass of curls. Lil's own hair was
stringing in rats' tails down her damp cheeks,
and her face was pale, while Nan's brown skin

was clear and her cheeks rose-coloured. It was no wonder Tony had noticed her, but——

"Tony," Lil whispered, "you said I was pretty the other day!"

"So you are," he returned, easily. "Say, we're humming along home now, aren't we?" glancing at Frank and the tiller.

"There's a boat. Oh," shrieked Nan, "it's Dick and Percy! Come about, Frank—quick! They're waiting under the lee of the land."

Loud were the jubilations as the two boys scrambled on board from a fisherman's boat, and great the rejoicing that they would be at home by eight after all. Nan waved a farewell hand at the fisherman who had rowed them out, as Percy and Dick explained what had delayed them. The boats had all been out, and they had had to wait for the first one back.

"And when I said I wanted a boat for Nan, old Jollimore came himself," Dick finished. "He said Nan looked after his wife all one summer when she was ill and he was on the Banks fishing."

"To-morrow's Nettie's party, Tony," said Lil, suddenly. "Tell me, are there any strangers coming?"

"Heaps," Tony returned, carelessly, and

stared at Nan. " Won't you come, Nan ? " he demanded.

" Me ? I've no dress," she responded, affably. " Thank you, all the same."

" It's an awful pity you're not going," Dick grumbled. " I shan't know any girls."

" You know Lil."

" Yes, but she won't bother about me. She'll be the prettiest one there. They'll all run after her."

" Of course," Nan assented, with unbounded admiration, " and her dress is *lovely*. Oh, Dick, be sure you tell me what there is for supper ! Nettie said the ices were coming from New York."

" What's that ? " Tony came and squeezed in between them.

Nan ostentatiously removed herself, but it was impossible for her to remain haughtily aloof for long, however much she wished to, and suddenly she laughed.

" I'm not going to spend the rest of our sail dodging you, Tony Yelverton," she observed, decidedly ; " but I'm not going to talk to you. So you just get away. I can't bear a mean boy, who just pretends to be a rescuer, and that's what you did."

" Nan, you *were* rude to Tony," Lil scolded,

6

when the boys had landed them on their own shore.

"I meant to be"—with contentment.   "He deserved it—he was mean.   Why, Lil Addington, you haven't got a spark of spirit!"

"What about you—when you told them all you couldn't go to Nettie's party because you hadn't a dress?"

"Well, it was true!"   Nan opened astonished eyes at her.

"It wasn't nice.   You're always telling people how poor we are, and I hate it."   Lil banged down the empty meat pie dish on the floor of the back porch.

"Sorry," Nan began, "I won't do it again," and forgot all about it as her mother called out a greeting.   "Oh, mummy, we had a splendid time.   I'll tell you about it.   Only say, first, that we're not late."

"Late?   You're on the stroke."

Mrs. Addington laughed as Nan bounced into the living-room, curly-haired and blooming. But Cousin Adelaide turned really pale at the day's adventure.

"Oh, Mary," she gasped, "you will never, never let them go again!"

"Oh, yes," said Mrs. Addington, coolly, "Why not?"

CHAPTER VII

LIL'S PARTY

LIL stood before her glass with a beating heart on the night of Nettie Yelverton's party.

Nan had had her innings yesterday out on the wet yacht, but to-night it was her turn. Her wonderful new dress lay on her bed, a glimmering mass of soft white *crepe de Chine* over white satin ; little white shoes and silk stockings lay by it, for Cousin Adelaide had forgotten nothing, even to a little string of real pearls for her throat.

Lil gasped with sheer pleasure as her mother finished doing her hair, clasped the new pearls round her soft white throat, and bade her look at herself. She had always known her hair was corn-yellow and her eyes blue, but she had never guessed one would look like a crown of gold and the other like sapphire stars over Cousin Adelaide's pearls and the white frock. She was almost solemn as she opened her door to go downstairs. Billy and the dogs sat there waiting to see her, Rose's head popped out of the kitchen ; even Cousin Adelaide clapped her hands softly as Lil came slowly down.

" You're simply a beauty, Lil Addington," Nan exclaimed, heartily. " You'll knock all the girls *cold* ! "

" Don't you wish you were coming too ? " demanded the heroine of the evening. " Oh, Billy, Doll's got my glove ! "

" Not a bit." Nan dived for Doll and the precious white glove. " I'm too sleepy," and Cousin Adelaide suddenly remembered Nan had been making a violet bed all day. " Here's your glove."

" Doll wouldn't have hurt it, he's very gentle," Billy said, hastily. " Even Hidigeigei, the Boarder, isn't any whiter nor fluffier than you, Lil. Please bring me home two ice-creams."

Lil laughed and went to the door, carrying her little slippers, for she had to walk only through the back garden to the Yelvertons'.

" If I were rich, Lil, you'd have a motor, even if you only had to go two yards," Nan cried.

" Wood will come for you at twelve. Have a lovely time, Lil, dear," Mrs. Addington said. " You do look sweet."

Lil waved her hand and disappeared, in a

dream of happiness and content that lasted till she had left her white shawl and her thick shoes in the dressing-room and sailed into the big drawing-room, cleared for the occasion. Then, in spite of her pearls and her white shoes, she came awake with a jerk.

Tony had said there would be strangers. To Lil, standing in the doorway, the whole middle of the big room seemed to be packed with nothing but strangers. There were girls, and girls, and girls, mixed with boys and really grown-up men ; but it was the girls Lil Addington looked at—girls in white lace, and apple-blossom tulle, and silver tissue ; one, very tall and striking, in leaf-green satin, with real emeralds round her neck. Lil knew suddenly why Cousin Adelaide had called her white frock " a little dress." It was only a little dress, next to these girls out of a fashion book—just a plain little dress. Lil wished furiously that Cousin Adelaide had let Miss Hunt cut the neck lower. All the other girls were *décolletée* ; not like her, just a schoolgirl in a schoolgirl's frock. She did not know a soul in the room, except Nettie and Tony Yelverton, and Nettie was too much engaged with her strange friends to take any notice of her. But Tony had asked her for five dances, and she could afford to wait for him.

So she greeted Mrs. Yelverton, secured a programme with a red pencil, and once more felt grown-up and important.

But Tony never came near her. He rushed by, with a large gardenia in his coat, flung her a good-natured " Hullo, Lil ! " and—that was all ! He never mentioned his five dances, nor wrote on her programme.

Lil stood stunned. No one introduced even a single partner to her. No one came to write on the brand new programme. The band struck up—that band from New York—and Nettie, every one but Lil, danced out down the polished floor. Tony whirled by her with the girl in the leaf-green dress, and without even a look. Lil, with her little feet thrilling to the music, realized suddenly that no one wanted her for a partner, nobody would have known if she had stayed at home. Only fat Mrs. Yelverton, a vast expanse of satin and diamonds, glanced at her uneasily, and asked if she would have some ice-cream or lemonade.

Lil declined, mechanically. She was afraid to move, afraid to walk over to a secluded corner by herself, past Tony, who had not come near her. But her anguish while the dancing was going on was nothing to what she felt when the music stopped, the room emptied, and she

stood on the wide floor alone. Even fat Mrs.
Yelverton had vanished—gone off to play
bridge and appear no more, now that her part
in the evening was off her mind. Lil, a small
white atom in the big room, stood there
speechless.

Frank Allen, arriving late, jerked up in the
dancing-room doorway, and beckoned to his
brother.

"Look there," said he, succinctly. "I knew
that cad Tony would round on her! Lil's
having a dreadful time! Tell Johnston Earlwood
I want him, and get some of the other boys.
We'll see Lil isn't left alone any more."

Lil saw him, and was afraid to look up, for
fear he might think she wanted him to dance
with her, but Frank was across the floor.

"Hullo, Lil, we're late too!" he began,
easily. "Come along and dance with some of
us, won't you? I say, your dress is perfectly
stunning!"

Lil surrendered the horrible empty programme, which she would rather have torn up
and trampled upon, and to her wild surprise suddenly found it more than half filled by half a
dozen boys who appeared with Dick Allen.

"My cousin—his name's Johnston Earlwood,"
said Dick, casually, of the eldest of them, who

was really a man and had finished at Harvard ; and Lil had never heard enough of any world but Happy Valley to know that Johnston Earlwood's father could have bought up the Yelvertons and never have missed the money.

Johnston Earlwood smiled down at the pretty schoolgirl with the yellow hair, and Lil smiled back with sudden gaiety. There was no standing out for her after that. She danced gaily for the rest of the evening, and was not even offended when she overheard an old gentleman inquire who the pretty child was in the white frock.

Supper was a dream of glory. Johnston Earlwood asked leave to come and call the next day ; Nettie Yelverton came over to Lil's table, as soon as she saw it surrounded five boys deep, with two hot-house peaches to be taken home for Billy. Miss Yelverton's conscience suddenly troubled her, not so much because she had forgotten Lil, but that behind Lil was the elegant Cousin Adelaide, who had ideas about manners.

"Do tell your cousin it was a nice party," she said, affectionately, as Lil bade her good night. "And you'll come to our picnic, won't you ? Bring your cousin too, to talk to mother. To-morrow, at three, don't forget."

But Lil, in spite of a dance that night and a picnic to-morrow, and Johnston Earlwood walking home with her to Wood's silent rage, went to bed and wept. Tony Yelverton had never come near her, had forgotten her; and it was only for Tony that she cared. She remembered the girl in green, and sobbed as she went to sleep. It was hopeless for Lil Addington with her one " little dress " to try and compete with the brilliant rich girls who made up Tony's set.

It was more hopeless still to have to pile downstairs early in the morning and pack and ticket vegetables for market, instead of breakfasting in bed in Cousin Adelaide's pale-blue wrapper. Lil's lip quivered as she helped Rose put the heavy baskets in the wagon for Nan to drive to the grocer who took most of their produce. But Nan came back with the empty wagon full of glee with her adventures.

" Fielding says he'll send you over a cheque at the end of the week, or will you take some of it in groceries ? " she inquired cheerfully. " And I met Dick and his cousin Johnston Earlwood, and they drove into town with me. They sat on the baskets and didn't mind a bit."

" Oh, Nan, and you in your awful hat ! Johnston Earlwood must have been mortified to death when he saw what we did for our living," Lil flashed, and despised herself the instant it was out.

"Not a bit! He's much too nice. He——"

But Cousin Adelaide cut Nan off. "Oh, Lil, dear," she begged, "do remember it doesn't matter a bit what you do—it's what you are!"

"Why, Cousin," Lil protested, "if we stole!"

"I wasn't speaking of doing wrong. I don't mind telling you I didn't like the idea of you children selling vegetables when first I came, but I see now I had a false ideal. You're gentlefolk, you can do as you like—and naturally Johnston Earlwood would understand that as well as I do. His father and mother are charming people."

Mrs. Addington nodded, glad Cousin Adelaide had spoken out to Lil, and turned at the sound of Rose's voice from the kitchen.

"Nan, see what Rose wants, will you?" she said, gently.

But Nan came back frowning. "Rose says——" she began and interrupted herself. "Oh, the Yelvertons want to know if we can let them have some lettuce, and I sent Wood over with it." Mrs. Addington never allowed either Nan or Lil to go with baskets to people's back doors. "Rose says what are we going

to do about keeping her? The Railway Hotel
has sent up to know if she'll go there."

"Oh!" Nan's mother flushed with distress.
"I don't know, Nan! I really think we can't
afford to keep Rose."

"Oh, mother, think how tired you get," Nan
begged. "Couldn't we manage—somehow—to
keep her?"

"I don't know, and I wouldn't like her to
lose a good place. Tell her I'll let her know
presently." Mrs. Addington turned bravely to
Cousin Adelaide. "You see, Rose is rather in
request."

But Cousin Adelaide had folded up her
embroidery and slipped away.

Rose was not surprised to see her coming into
the kitchen. The two were great friends,
Cousin Adelaide thinking and saying Rose was
the best cook she had ever known, and Rose
finding the guest a mine of new hints and
recipes. "What's this, Rose, about the Railway Hotel wanting you?" Cousin Adelaide
inquired, sitting down.

"Well, they've been sending every day,
and I felt as if I'd have to give 'em some kind
of an answer. But I'd not leave Mrs. Addington
for any money if she'd keep me. Only she
thinks she can't afford to pay me, and I can't

work without wages. Oh, I won't be going till
you go "—reassuringly. " I wouldn't be real
mean to Mrs. Addington while she had company
—let alone your being here was the only reason
I came."

" But how will they manage all winter
without you ? "

" Dunno," Rose ruminated. " Of course
they've had to before this. But with the girls
at school most all day it comes hard on Mrs.
Addington, and I dunno if you've noticed she
ain't looking real well. I'd give a deal to stay ;
but there—it's just Mrs. Addington hasn't the
money."

" That needn't stop you." Cousin Adelaide
was quite pale. " I won't deceive you, Rose; I
came out to see if you could arrange to stay
here for the winter. I would be responsible
for your wages."

Emotion and Rose were strangers, but for
once her answer was husky. " That's real good
of you. And it won't be forgot to you. But "
—she waved a hand toward the living-room—
" you'll have to tell her."

" I'll tell her. And Rose "—Cousin Adelaide
lowered her voice—" I want you to let me know
if Mrs. Addington doesn't look better after I
leave."

" Sure," Rose affirmed, " though I ain't much at writing. If you don't hear from me you'll know things is progressing suitably for her. Billy, it's near dinner time," as a curly head came round the kitchen door. "You be a good boy, and get cleaned up. And you and me'll have a fine time this afternoon while the others is at the picnic ! "

" I think they might have asked a little boy," Cousin Adelaide remarked, incautiously, mindful of lamentation that morning.

Billy nodded. " I howled," he confessed. " But, you see, there's that way we've all got to walk on, and mummy 'minded me about the palace of the king, and I was sorry I made a fuss."

" What palace ? "

" It's in his story-book," Rose explained. " Just a story ! "

" It's not," Billy contradicted, hotly. " It's true—only I forgot about it."

" Well, if he isn't a funny child," Rose confided, as Billy disappeared to be washed. " When he talks so good I feel as if he's going to die young, only I get relieved right away when he eats up all the cake I'm saving for Sunday. I'll make him a gingerbread soon's you all get off."

Cousin Adelaide thought he, was probably superintending it as she followed Mrs. Addington and the girls to the shore. Certainly there was no sign of him about the house once he had kissed his mother good-bye. The girls never thought of him, in the excitement of finding an electric launch to take them across the bay with the rest of the Yelvertons' guests, and in the way the Yelvertons had translated the plain word picnic. The servants had arrived before them and done everything, from the fire to laying the table. Nan was deciding she much preferred her hardworking outings with the Allen boys to this elegantly dull entertainment, when Nettie Yelverton took her arm.

"Come down to the shore, Nan," she demanded. "Mother wants me to see if there is anybody else coming. Wasn't it perfectly horrid, we never knew till this morning that Johnston Earlwood was Perry Earlwood's son —the steel magnate, you know—and not just those Allen boys' cousin? His father and mother are staying at Bear Bay, on their way to Newport, so of course as soon as Mother found out she telephoned for them to come to-day. But so far they haven't. Why on earth didn't Lil tell us last night about Johnston?"

"I don't believe she knew then." Nan

stared. "But I don't see what difference it can make. Johnston's nice."

"You mean he admires Lil," Nettie snapped. "I don't think she's so frightfully pretty, and neither does Tony. He says you could be far better-looking if you liked—just fascinating!"

"I'd rather go to college than be pretty," Nan laughed, unimpressed.

"Why, Nan Addington, what an idea!" Nettie stood still in amazement. "Being pretty's everything. You can nearly always get married the first year you come out. And going to college is so *stuffy*. Besides, you'd be miserable at any college unless somebody gave you a huge allowance—the girls are so sniffy if you don't have proper clothes!"

"I want to go, all the same"—obstinately.

But Nettie was not listening.

"My heavens," she shrieked, "it's them! It's the Perry Earlwoods. "Mamma thought they must have missed the launch, and here they are now in a dirty old boat, with an awful little boy rowing them. Mamma'll be wild."

Nan stood paralysed. Sure enough a fat, elderly gentleman and a lady, exquisitely dressed in the same kind of white stuff as Cousin Adelaide, were getting out of a dilapidated old boat within five yards of her, where a grubby little urchin had just shipped his oars.

Nettie Yelverton was showering protestations on them at the top of her voice. Her mother would be simply mortified that they had missed the launch and had to come like this.

" Not at all, not at all," Mr. Perry Earlwood returned, cheerfully. " We've had lots of fun."

" In that dirty old boat—that smells of fish ! " gasped Nettie.

" It was quite clean, my dear, and the little boy rowed beautifully ; he said he had been rowing most of his life." Mrs. Earlwood gathered up her spotless skirts and got out. " Give him a quarter, Perry ; ten cents is not enough for convoying two large people like us ! "

But as the Perry Earlwoods disappeared towards Mrs. Yelverton with the profusely apologetic Nettie, Nan never stirred. The little boy in the boat had turned and winked at her, and he was Billy—Billy at his dirtiest, in his worst clothes, masquerading as a ferry boy in Wood's old boat and taking money from strangers. Nettie had not recognized him— she had little care for small boys. But what would his mother say ?

" Go home, Billy, at once," Nan commanded, in a fierce undertone.

"Yes'm," said Billy, in the voice of Rose, and chuckled. "I've got a lot-er-money, Nan, I've got forty cents!"

"That won't do you any good if Cousin Adelaide sees you. Fly!"

His sister chuckled as she looked after him, toiling valiantly back to his dogs and Rose. Poor Billy, and his lot-er-money; poor wee man! Nan might laugh, but her eyes were misty as she went back to the picnic and the ice-cream Billy might just as well have had too.

7

CHAPTER VIII

"HE CAN SWIM"

An air of languor hung over the Addington family on the morning after the Yelvertons' picnic. There had been dancing after the outdoor dinner, and it was midnight when they reached home, to find Billy clutching his forty cents, even when wrapped in slumber.

Mrs. Addington was tired, and for once sat still and did nothing; Cousin Adelaide maintained an air of aloofness, which disapproved of the Yelverton family and all their works; Lil had found the evening too wonderful and beautiful to say much about it; only Nan announced frankly that she had enjoyed herself.

"It was perfectly heavenly, once you realized you wouldn't have to wash a dish," she announced, when they all sat on the veranda. "Why, Billy Boy, what have you got there?"

Billy toiled up the path to the veranda, bare-legged and water-splashed, but such slight disadvantages never deterred him from joining his family.

" Fish." He held up three diminutive morsels. " They're for Cousin Adelaide."

" Oh, Billy, and you caught them ? How splendid of you. We'll take them in to Rose to be cooked for my dinner," said the fortunate recipient. " But aren't you back rather early ? It's only half-past ten, and you don't usually arrive till the stroke of dinner ! "

" I know," Billy assented, gloomily.

" Where's Tommy Yelverton ? " Nan inquired.

" Gone home." The family's disinclination for conversation seemed to have spread even to Billy.

Lil waved a languid fan, Nan wondered for the fortieth time if her mother would let her help in Nettie Yelverton's theatricals, and when she had better ask her, and Billy cast himself suddenly on his mother's lap.

" He can swim ! " he exploded, darkly.

" Who can ? " Mrs. Addington inquired, easily.

" Mr. Yelverton."

" He means Tony," said Nan, scornfully. " He isn't Mr. Yelverton, Billy."

" I don't," Billy returned, stolidly. " I mean the father Yelverton. The great, big, fat mountain Mr. Yelverton. You never saw anything so queer as he was, all doubled up in the water, till he looked like a rolled-up crab. But he swam very, very well."

"How did he get into the water?" Nan demanded, staring.

"He fell in, out of a boat."

"But how?"—impatiently.

"He got hooked on the line of a fishing-rod," Billy returned, with sudden loquacity. "He got caught, and he sort of dodged. I was fishing on the landing and he came along in the dinghy and drifted past—and I don't *think* I hit him with my pole when he dodged about my hook, but out he went with such a plop—smash, smack into the water! I didn't truly see, because just about that time I thought I'd better be coming home with Cousin's fish, and I did."

"Why, Billy Boy," gasped his mother, "wasn't he very angry?"

"His words sounded dreadful loud, and he swallowed a nawful lot of salt water and looked very funny," Billy faltered, gloomily. "It didn't seem to be any kind of a time for saying I didn't mean to!"

"Oh, dear, shall I have to go and apologize?" Mrs. Addington had no desire to leave her chair.

"I'm going myself," Billy announced, with some misgiving. "I s'pose he can only talk loud at me."

"Good, brave boy," Cousin Adelaide observed proudly, as he departed. "Really, Mary, it must have been dreadfully funny. I should have enjoyed seeing that fat man in the water —oh, yes, I should! You are doing quite the right thing in going at once, Billy."

Billy paused with one foot on the path. "Well, you see, I have to, Cousin Adelaide," he rejoined with engaging candour. "You see I left my hook stuck in him, and I'm afraid he may be so boiling angry he'll break my rod!"

Even Cousin Adelaide gave way to laughter as he disappeared.

"You sound very cheerful," said Dick Allen, suddenly appearing round the house with Johnston Earlwood. "May we come and call?"

Mrs. Addington laughed and assured them they were welcome to Idletown—her greatest ambition was to collect lazy people.

"What's your greatest ambition, Dick?" Nan asked idly, as he sat down by her.

"To be a big mining engineer"—calmly. "When I've made lots of money, Nan, I'll come back, and we'll have a fine time. I'll get a new yacht and we'll go to Europe."

"What kind of mining will you do—gold mines?"

"Gold, coal, all kinds"—with reckless grandeur. "I've got to do a lot of hard work first though. I'm going away next week, Nan; but I hope I'll be back for Thanksgiving. What are you going to do yourself all winter?"

"Learn dressmaking"—Nan replied, with a glance at Cousin Adelaide. Dressmaking was the last knowledge Nan wanted, in spite of Lil's request to Cousin Adelaide. There was no sense in it, she said to herself hotly; she never went anywhere to wear fine clothes. And to sit in a hot room over patterns when Cousin might so easily have made her present books, or even a nest-egg for the longed-for college—— Nan bit her lip and brought herself up sharply. "Cousin thinks I ought to learn to cut out."

"Oh, don't!" Dick besought her, laughing. "You can cut out all the girls already. Hullo, here's Billy! I thought you'd have got eaten, Bill, by that big fish you caught!"

Billy shook his head. "I did it, though," he testified. "I said Mother says I am dreadful sorry, Mr. Yelverton, and he said *G-r-r-r*! He didn't seem to have liked the water much, though I told him he swam beautifully. He called me 'You dreadful little boy!'"

He smiled affably at Dick's roar of laughter, and sat down unnoticed at Johnston Earlwood's feet with a large bowl of water, in which swam Cousin Adelaide's latest present, two boats and a covey of ducks. But the magnet with which Billy usually drew them round the basin at top speed was absent, and he gazed suddenly at Johnston Earlwood.

"You're not a magnet," Billy reproached him with shrill disappointment. "They said you were—but my ducks aren't even *moving*."

"Not a *what*?" responded the astonished Johnston.

"A magnet. Tommy Yelverton told me you were a steel magnet, and I've brought down all the things in my bowl and you don't draw them a bit. I thought such a big magnet as you would drag them right out of the water!"

He clutched his mother as the others laughed, and Mrs. Addington kissed him.

"Oh, Billy Boy, Johnston isn't a magnet," she said, softly. "Tommy said a magnate, and he meant Johnston's father. It's just a word for a very powerful man. Why don't you go and find the dogs? I haven't seen Hidigeigei this morning."

"His name isn't Hidigeigei any more," Billy returned, wrathfully. "He won't answer

to it. When I was finished fishing this morning
I called him to come home quick, and he went
and stayed to watch Mr. Yelverton land.
He's going to be Boarder again."

"Never you mind, Billy, he's a real crackajack of a dog anyhow," said Dick, consolingly.
"Now, ladies, vacation's soon going to end,
so Johnston's come to ask you to a good-
bye party."

"All of us?" Lil cried, rapturously.

"Mrs. Addington's the first and most important guest," Johnston affirmed, smiling.
"Would Tuesday suit you, Mrs. Addington?"

"Oh, Johnston, I'm afraid—I've too much to
do"—Mrs. Addington hesitated.

"Then there won't be any party, and we'll
all be disappointed," returned the wily Johnston.

Mrs. Addington laughed, and gave in, and
Johnston poured out details. The party was
to be at Bear Bay, where there were sands and
surf bathing, and two automobiles would take
them there.

"Mummy, can I go?" Billy broke out.

"Dead cert, Billy," Johnston nodded. "I
thought we'd start at eleven on Tuesday morning
if you approved, Mrs. Addington. The day
can be altered, but the party can't be. Never!
There'll be ten of us: you and Mrs. Sinclair,

Lil and Nan, Dick, Frank, and myself, and I'll ask Nettie and Tony Yelverton. Billy, of course ; and I think we can tuck that Tommy Yelverton in somewhere."

Billy precipitated himself on him. " Haven't you a shorter name than Johnston ? " He demanded. " Johnston's so long to take to a picnic."

" I'm called Jack at home," replied the host, agreeably.

Billy shook his head. " I think," he pondered solemnly, " I'll call you Magnet ! "

" Billy," reproved his mother, " he mayn't like it."

Johnston Earlwood laughed. " I'm deeply complimented, Mrs. Addington. I only wish it were true."

Mrs. Addington rather thought it was. She herself was going to a picnic for the second time in a week, and even Cousin Adelaide was coolly excited. The girls lived in a frenzy of packing vegetables and despatching them, pressing dresses, and making jam, so as to have a clear day on Tuesday. Even Nan retrimmed her big straw hat, and Rose kept her mouth closed on the gloomy prophecy that Tuesday was sure to be foggy.

But Tuesday was brilliant. Johnston

Earlwood appeared at the door with an enormous borrowed Cadillac which held everybody, as more sociable than two cars, and Mrs. Addington paused wildly as she was getting into it. Billy, Doll, and the sedulously washed Boarder occupied the best seats in the tonneau.

"Oh, Billy, the dogs can't go!" she gasped. "They would be a trouble."

Billy all but burst into tears. "They must go; I promised them," he wailed. "I told them they were going!"

"They were specially invited, if you and Mrs. Sinclair don't mind," Johnston Earlwood whispered. "All right, Billy! Dog family can take their seats."

Nettie Yelverton could have lived without them. They conducted a loud yapping match all through the village, hanging precariously over the side of the car from Billy's clutch on their tails, while they roared defiance at each dog on the road. In the country they scrambled frantically from one side to the other and over every one's lap. Cousin Adelaide and Nan good-naturedly allowed themselves to be trampled on, and Nettie Yelverton's complaints were unheard.

Miss Yelverton had on her very best clothes, and her most elegant manner. After one attempt

to talk in whispers to Johnston Earlwood and
ignore the rest of the party, and finding his
attention bestowed on Billy's naughty dogs and
Mrs. Addington's comfort, she had subsided
into a silent stare. Mrs. Addington, to the girl,
was just old and shabbily dressed, but somehow it dawned on Nettie slowly that she was
all wrong. Mrs. Addington was almost pretty,
and she was talking about people and things
as Nettie herself could never have done. But
all the same——

" I should think you and all Mrs. Addington's
relations would hate her selling vegetables for a
living," she informed Cousin Adelaide, smartly.

Cousin Adelaide's eyes flashed. She did not
answer, which she trusted would be accounted
to her for virtue, but Nettie had seen the flash
and remembered her mother wanted the Honourable Mrs. Sinclair to come to their dinners in
the winter. So she wisely subsided once more.

Tony Yelverton too found things not quite
to his liking. No one paid any attention to
him where he was crowded in between Dick
and Frank Allen, nor listened when he observed
Bear Bay was not much of a place.

" I think it's *lovely*," Nan shrieked, as they
ploughed through a sandy road out on hard
sands. " Oh, look at the sea ! "

Before them stretched a wide bay directly open to the broad Atlantic, with great green rollers booming in over the hard yellow sands. At sight of them even Tony Yelverton forgot the languid airs he thought a college man should assume, and Nettie pinned up her expensively unsuitable muslin dress without even saying that it didn't matter if she spoiled it, since she had plenty more at home.

Billy, Nan, every one, raced down after the big wash of the undertow, and back again, with wild shrieks as the incoming roller gained on them.

" Isn't it erlirious ? " Billy screamed ; and it certainly was.

Cousin Adelaide privately thought lunch was delirious too, Johnston Earlwood had brought so much more than could possibly be eaten. But Nan beamed on him as she stoked the fire and made the coffee, proudly and expertly. Only on Billy was lunch lost. He could scarcely eat from excitement, and galloped off even before the ice-cream with the ecstatic Doll and Boarder, all three shrieking themselves hoarse as they tore madly up and down the beach after the unimpressed sandpipers.

Only Mrs. Addington and Cousin Adelaide were content to rest. The rest departed on

Billy's tracks to the sea, headed by Tony and the Magnet, whom no human being would ever have believed was twenty-three years old. Billy fell down and was soaked, of course, but to his surprise his mother produced a whole dry outfit, into which he was promptly hustled. But, alas! just before tea he slipped on a slimy stone and was grabbed out of the undertow by his ever-watchful host. Even the cheerful Billy was cast down, till his mother took off his outer garments and dressed him in her own long golf-coat, in which he promenaded with the greatest glee. But going home he succumbed, and slept placidly in a roll of rugs, with the exhausted dog retinue slumbering beside him.

Tony Yelverton sat next Lil on the way home. Johnston Earlwood's admiration for her had not been wasted on Tony, and he was not going to be cut out by him. He congratulated himself on his success as he talked to Lil in whispers during the twilight drive, his voice covered by the songs all the others were singing.

"You have had a good time, haven't you, Lil?" he asked, as the motor stopped at the Addingtons' door.

"Not as nice as at your party, Tony," said

Lil, sweetly. "You see, I had a heavenly escape there of those five dances you never came for! Good night."

Tony was speechless. Nan's voice rose over her mother's as she thanked Johnston Earlwood.

"It was the best party I ever went to—perfectly great."

But Lil's head was in a whirl as she went indoors. She had snubbed Tony Yelverton as hard as she could, and to her wild surprise she was glad of it!

CHAPTER IX

THE WAY OUT

THERE was a lull after these glorious picnics, and Nan remarked dreamily: "Sometimes I feel as if I'd like to be the girl that doesn't have to, though I'm frightfully proud of this year's strawberry crop. It was a record, and all those new plants I put out did come on well. We're going to take a lot more runners this year, mummy. And you see we'll break the record again."

"I'm glad we don't have to plant them out till later," observed Lil. "The Earlwoods haven't gone away, and working in the garden makes me dreadfully sunburnt."

"You're getting so grown-up you'll be finding a grey hair soon," laughed Nan. "Parties are lovely. I could go to one every day. I'm tired of working."

"Cousin Adelaide's got some lovely stuff for sunburn"—Billy smiled at them—" tastes nice too. I licked it. It was on my cracked lip.

It's called ' Seem No.' You ask her for it, Lil."

" What does he mean ? " demanded Lil.

" That's its name," stated the little boy. " She told me it was."

" Cousin Adelaide," asked Lil, as Mrs. Sinclair came through the hall, "what's ' Seem No ' ? Billy says you have it to cure sunburn."

" ' Crême Simon,' " laughed Cousin, " and I put some on his sore lip. I'm going now to consult Rose about what we'll have to eat when Annabel comes. Your mother will tell you who she is."

" I never heard of her, mummy. Who is she ? " and Lil turned to her mother.

" She's Lady Annabel Sinclair, and is coming to see Cousin. She'll stay at the Railway Hotel," replied Mrs. Addington.

" Mother, how perfectly heavenly ! Lady Annabel." Lil murmured the name again. " Think of her coming here." Lil knew she'd be beautiful and golden-haired. Oh, how much the girl wished she'd been born Lady Annabel or even Lady Lilian ! " Is she related to Cousin ? "

" To Mr. Sinclair," answered Mrs. Addington. " Isn't it a mercy we've got Rose to cook ? We'll have to entertain her and have her here for meals."

" Oh, mother ! "—Nan's eyes shone—" do let
us take summer boarders ; we might get the
kind they have in books. Think how lovely
it would be to have a great heiress here. They'd
put pictures in the papers, and she'd be elderly
—old really ; maybe she'd adopt us, and——"
" Don't listen to her, mother," Lil begged
with a puckered forehead, frowning crossly.
" Boarders would be worse than anything. As
if a garden and selling vegetables wasn't enough.
Why, people despise—well, look down on us
anyway, and if we had boarders——"
" You are a nasty little snob," interrupted
Nan. But she wasn't angry, only laughing.
" Boarder'll get boarders," retorted Billy.
" Wasn't I calling him hard the other day, and
there were some queer-looking people going by,
and they did like me and called ' Boarder,
Boarder ! that's the way they get them in
down here.' Do they mother ?   Do they ? "
" There now," said Lil, while the others
laughed. " How on earth would we feed and
amuse them ? "
" They'd amuse themselves," replied Nan.
" You just let them have a boat and do as they
like."
" But do they get boarders in like that ? "
persisted Billy ; " do they?"

8

"No," answered his mother. "Of course they were laughing."

"Promise me, mother, you won't let Nan think of doing such a crazy thing, will you?" besought Lil. "She's quite capable of going down to that little hotel and offering to let rooms to strangers."

"No, I'm not."

"I'd be even more mortified than I am now," said Lil. "Why, Nettie says most people can't think how we work as we do. And she says lots of people she knows would pay to get introduced to Cousin."

"Lil, that's dreadful," remarked her mother. "Don't listen to such ill-bred things."

"Well, she married an 'honourable' and belongs to one of the oldest New York families," maintained Lil, though she did look rather ashamed.

"Why, Lil Addington, you get worse and worse," said Nan. "You're talking exactly like Nettie."

"Well, you're dreadfully unkind," reproached Lil. "You tell every one what we do. Even the Earlwoods asked me how much we'd charge to supply them with violets every week. I was cold with mortification. I——"

"You want shaking," said Nan. "But I

can't see why we shouldn't take Lady Annabel
as a meal boarder anyway. We have to work
and we might just as well get paid for it,
and——"

" Nan ! "—Mrs. Addington's voice was almost
stern. Nan jumped. " You musn't say that.
After all Cousin's kindness, it's ungrateful. Of
course we'll do anything we can for any friend
of hers."

"Not ungrateful," mumbled Nan, " only,
mummy, you see, the things Cousin Adelaide
wants to do for me I don't really want. I don't
like them, and——"

" You're just horrid ; do go away." Lil was
indignant.

" I will," returned Nan, and unheeding her
mother's soft remonstrance, dashed off. She
was angry—tired too, and sick of everything ;
so she captured a good lunch when Rose wasn't
looking, grabbed a book she was dying to finish,
and departed to the hayloft over the old barn.
She vowed she'd stay there all day, and that's
what she'd do. They could get on without her,
omitting to remind herself of the fact that Lil
was going to the Yelvertons' and her mother
would do all the things that Nan had left
undone.

The lunch was excellent, and Nan ate it undisturbed by the calling of Lil. Then Billy wandered about shrieking, "Nan! Nannie!" Finally he too went away. They had never thought of the hayloft. Nan chuckled. Then she reminded herself she was angry. Lil was a pig, and mother hadn't stood up for Nan as she might have. No, it didn't matter what they wanted, she'd stay where she was. Lost in her story, Nan sprawled on the hay. It was comfortable, and she was glad she had disregarded the various voices that called sharply, pleadingly. Let them know where she'd hidden? Not much. And then she went to sleep.

She woke with a start. That noise on the roof was rain. Why, it was pouring hard—cold too; she felt chilly. The loft was getting dark, there were mice scampering about; she hated mice. That surely was a rat, or was it a bat? Poor Nan was too panicky to notice particularly. This was where she'd be getting away from the loft. She'd had more than enough of it and snatched her book and started to go down. She'd find her mother at once and tell her how sorry she was having left all those things for her to do. There were clean covers to put in Cousin Adelaide's bedroom and some silver which Nan had promised to polish and—oh, fifty things! She was suffering from remorse and regret. But, oh my! where was that ladder? She'd come up by it. But it wasn't there—*it wasn't there*! She peered down into the gloom below. Somebody had taken away that ladder while she slept, and she had never heard a sound. What on this earth could she do now? Stay up there all night? Why, they'd all be simply crazy about her, they'd be terrified, thinking something awful must have happened to her. Would anyone hear if she called? That wasn't likely, but still she'd try it. So—though the rain came in on her through the open window—she stood there calling, calling till she was hoarse. But no one answered her. Then she had sense enough to realize that the open window was letting rain in and she'd better push the hay back; if the winter food for the pony was ruined—well, things would be worse than ever.

Piling hay up was hot work, but it was something to do. Better than sitting waiting for the dark to come down and for mice an rats to come out—perhaps bats! Ugh! Nan shuddered. While collecting the hay into heap she struck something hard. Deciding sh might as well investigate, she found it was table. Pushing the hay away from it, as fa as she could see it wasn't much good—just a

ordinary round table with claw legs and dirty;
my goodness, but that table was filthy! Just
as if it had been under a tap one day and in a
sandstorm the next. Well, it wasn't any use
as far as she could see. Unless—could she
drop it down through the trap-door where the
ladder used to come up? Oh, that ladder,
where had it gone? If she could do that and
let herself down on to the table, then she'd be
able to get out somehow. The loft was a little
lighter, the rain not so heavy. She had no idea
of the time, and didn't own a watch. Tugging
her find along—it was heavy and very solid—she
began to weep, just a few painful tears. What
a beast she'd been!

"Nan Addington, you plain idiot!" she
scolded herself. "Get that table along and
try to get down by it."

She pulled it as far as the trap-door, but it
wouldn't go through. The table was round—
rounder than the long, narrow opening. There
it stuck, the hateful thing. After trying it
sideways and every other kind of way, and
getting blazing hot, she pushed it back—as a
substitute for a ladder it was no good—and sat
down to think. There must be some way of
getting out if only she could think of it.
She'd be sure to hurt herself if she jumped.

Better to stay there all night till Wood came in the morning and face fifty rats than break an arm or a leg and give mother all that extra worry.

Suddenly she remembered seeing Wood throw the hay straight down into the pony's stall. Well now, there must be a hole from the loft. Where was it ? If found, could she get through it ?

It took some time, but at last she discovered it and wondered if she could slip down it. If the hayrack in the stall was fastened up at the lower end there, she'd be neither out nor in, but it was worth trying.

She pulled her skirts tight around her, held her arms close to her sides, and—dropped. It was a tight squeeze ; she felt afraid of sticking, and then that she'd smother and never get down. It was sort of dark and nasty too. Luckily she was very slight, and at last slid into the hayrack and—oh, joy !—it wasn't stopped up. With one spring she was down. Her clothes were filthy, her hair and face covered with dust and spiders' webs, and Nan—who feared spiders ever since that day a huge one dropped down her back, and Lil squashed it with a slap, and Nan felt the horrid thing on her skin—never even gave them a thought nor bothered about the horrid tickling webs that clung to her.

Where was the pony ? The stall was empty.

The barn-door wasn't locked; and then she remembered. Mother and Cousin Adelaide had driven down to meet what Billy called the " Lady Cousin." That was it.

Nan began to hope they hadn't worried about her. They'd have gone out; perhaps they hadn't even missed her. By this time she was shaking. She was so sorry; could she ever be sorry enough for her wicked, wicked temper, for all those hateful angry thoughts of Mother and Lil, and—worst of all—her selfish treatment of Mother?, It had nothing to do with Nan Addington that Mother hadn't been toiling all that afternoon, doing the work that Nan ought to have done. It was just chance. And wasn't Nan thankful ! She threw herself down on the clean straw and just lay there.

But it was no good to feel like this, so she made a dash for the house. The rain was coming on heavier now, and, soaking wet and very dirty, Nan hoped to escape Rose's eagle eye. But no such luck. And the scream Rose gave brought Billy.

" Why Nan, what have you been doing ? " demanded Rose. " Ain't you been to Mrs. Yelverton's ? They sent up for you. Ain't you ? "

" Oh, Rose, help me," implored Nan, " do."

It wasn't often Nan asked for help. She was independent. Fifty times a day Lil would beg Rose to mend her clothes, to iron shirt-waists, to press dresses; but Nan—this was unusual.

Rose bit off the angry words and followed the girl upstairs.

"A bath and wash your hair," she said.

"I know. Oh, Rose!" and Nan, speechless, hugged her.

"What's the matter? Where have you been? My sakes, ain't you black!"

"I was a beast," Nan gulped, "I got angry and I ran away and hid and——"

"You took my cookies and a turnover," accused Rose. "All this day I've been wondering where on earth they'd gone. I thought Billy had 'em, though I knew that child would er said if he had, and——"

"Mother didn't worry about me, did she?" interrupted Nan. "I'll tell her all about it, but——"

"Gimme your clothes," ordered the capable one. "Why did you go off like that in such a tear?"

"Because I was so angry."

"Billy was looking all around for you and I said you'd gone to Mrs. Yelverton's."

" I was up in the hayloft and someone pulled away the ladder and I couldn't get down."

" Land sakes ! "

" At last I came down the hayrack and out by the pony's manger."

Rose nodded. " Least said," she remarked, pointedly. Nan looked dreadfully white, so Rose brought her up a cup of coffee and made her drink it while she dressed. Then Nan set to work and put everything straight that she should have done in the morning. She felt as if she had been away for months and sort of shocked too. Could she have been in such a dreadful passion ? She realized it with deep, deep shame.

Her mother said very little when she came back, and Nan told her how sorry she was, and related how she had made an exit from the loft. The girl looked really worn out and went to bed early.

Mrs. Addington sat and sewed while waiting for Lil, who was with the Yelvertons', and Cousin Adelaide, who had stayed to dinner with the " Lady Cousin." It was getting late for Lil to be out, and her mother felt uneasy.

" Mrs. Addington "—there was Rose with her hat on and wearing a warm coat—" just going over to bring Miss Lil home. She's out pretty late."

Mrs. Addington nodded. Rose was a comfort. Suddenly she heard a motor and Cousin Adelaide's voice and Lil's.

"Why, Rose has gone to the Yelvertons' for you, Lil," said her mother.

Lil mumbled something, and it sounded as if she said, "Treating me as if I were a baby," and with a short "good night" went upstairs.

"Mary, I can't bear that Yelverton boy," said Cousin Adelaide. "He had a party at the hotel. Lil was there. Such a rowdy, bad-style lot. And Lil—somehow I think Lil ought to go away."

"I don't see how she can," answered Mrs. Addington. "I don't care much for Tony, but mercifully neither he nor his family are here always."

Hearing Rose in the kitchen she went to tell her Lil was back.

Nan was sound asleep when her sister went into their room, and Lil was dreadfully disappointed. She wanted Nan to hear all about the party. Nettie had decided it would be much more fun to have dinner at an hotel; it was a sudden impulse. How perfectly heavenly to be able to afford expensive impulses! They'd danced, and Lil had had a splendid time. Oh, and she had seen Lady Annabel, who wasn't a bit like Lil expected—not really a beauty. But Nettie had been most frightfully impressed, and Lady Annabel did look distinguished and very proud.

But she didn't seem at all proud when she came early next morning to have breakfast with the Addingtons. Nan liked her. The girl still looked a bit white and she hugged her mother and asked what she wanted her to do. Wood had found the ladder by the apple-trees, but none had been taken, and Nan vowed she'd get even with the Marsh and Allen boys. It wasn't funny leaving her to climb down like that.

" But you can't say nasty things to them, for they did pick the strawberries for us and the cows didn't eat them," reminded Lil.

Nan remembered her anger and looked grave.

" No," she said, " I won't get cross, but it was a mean thing to do."

Billy was kept in bed because he had a slight chill.

" Too much of Rose's layer-cake," laughed Cousin Adelaide, but Billy affirmed it wasn't. And Rose said it was Mrs. Sinclair's candy, and Billy announced it was from eating porridge, and he wasn't going to have any that morning.

He always hated porridge, and the doctor ordered him to eat some for breakfast. The little boy evaded this sometimes, but this morning every one was determined that he'd just got to have it.

"You'll never grow big and strong if you don't," said Cousin.

Lady Annabel, who came to visit him, said the same. Billy thought she was kind, but he couldn't like her as much as he did Cousin. Lady Annabel said she knew lots of stories to tell him.

She knew he was a good boy and would eat all his porridge, especially if she told him a story. For he had slept very late and the others had finished their breakfast long before he awoke. Rose had brought up his tray, and Lady Annabel was sure if they'd all leave her alone with him she knew he'd eat porridge for her. She proceeded to tell him a story, kneeling down by the side of his bed. He was occupied with the porridge, and Lady Annabel talked away sweetly. She couldn't see very well, but only wore glasses for reading, so didn't notice very quickly; and she was deeply absorbed in the story.

The Addingtons listened for sounds of argument, but, hearing none, scattered to do the ordinary day's routine. Then Lady Annabel opened the bedroom door and announced proudly that he'd eaten nearly all of it.

" The dear little boy !   I knew I could manage him.   It was so simple." Having no children of her own, of course she knew much more than any real mother about their management. It was Nan who saw her first, and before the girl could shriek—she certainly opened her mouth— Cousin Annabel grabbed the stranger.

" Annabel !   Annabel ! " she exclaimed.

Nan subsided on the stairs and smothered her laughter. Mrs. Addington, running up, caught sight of Lady Annabel being propelled into the bathroom by Cousin.   Oh ! that little imp Billy, listening intently to the story, had deposited a large portion of the detested food of the top of her head.   Also, he had managed to spatter an oatmeal halo round her face. The poor lady—so pleased with her success— had no idea how she looked.   And—a deadly secret—she wore some false hair, so she hadn't felt the warm poultice on her head.

Nan and Mrs. Addington retired to laugh unheard.

" How on earth," gasped the girl, " will Cousin ever get it off ?   She'll need *sandpaper* ! "

" What I want to know is how did Billy ever get it *on* ? " laughed Mrs. Addington.

And for some time afterwards Lady Annabel was firmly convinced that the younger Addington girl had something queer about her. Why was she always laughing? Mrs. Addington's warning of " steady Nan, steady," seemed to be needed, while Cousin Adelaide's laughing eyes inspired fresh merriment in the girl—but no one mentioned Billy or oatmeal.

Lady Annabel liked Lil best.

Nan disappeared after dinner with Nettie Yelverton and the Allen and Marsh boys. There was a great deal of talking and laughing up in the garret and running up and down stairs. The house was quiet when Mrs. Sinclair and Lady Annabel went for a walk.

" They are dears, all the Addingtons," said Cousin Adelaide. " Full of mischief and fun, but it's harmless." She wasn't sure even now whether Annabel knew how Billy had decorated her. The removal of the porridge had been difficult. Oatmeal does stick—and that false hair! Lady Annabel, greatly surprised, stared at the speaker. Adelaide had always avoided young people. It was strange to hear her praise them. " They are very high-spirited but there's nothing underhand nor a mean bone in one of them."

" Yes," agreed the visitor.

She enjoyed her walk. It was a perfect day, so was the view across the inlet.

Strolling back to the house past the denuded strawberry beds Annabel, startled, turned, and there, coming towards her from the woods, was a yelling horde, waving sticks, pistols, beating drums, and shrieking. Annabel, wild with sudden uncontrollable panic, gave a screech and ran. But the quicker she went the quicker that crowd pursued her. What were they clamouring?

" Death to the paleface! "

Faster went the terrified one, leaving Mrs. Sinclair far behind—faster followed the pursuers. The open door of the woodshed offered sanctuary and into it tore Annabel.

Shouts of " Scalps! " increased her terror. Those carefully treasured hair aids—would they take them? She sank down on the woodpile and hardly dared breathe. Hiding her face, she expected every moment to be seized by the hair and lose her most precious possessions ; but the noise passed by! She crouched, waiting hours—really a few moments : they had gone—she was alone in the shed. At last she ventured to sit up and look round. Then she crept out. No one was in sight. Sighing with relief, she straightened her dress and brushed off the dust of the wood-pile ; and then Adelaide came round the corner arm-in-arm with the leader of the band, and before Annabel could utter a word she was grabbed and hugged by Nan, who carried a drum. Nettie was beating a tin tray and making an unearthly noise ; and then a crowd collected from the garden.

Wasn't Lady Annabel a peach to run like that ? To pretend to be terrified ? Why, she looked just as if she'd thought they were real Indians. Where had she hidden ? How had they missed her ? Some of the others were running yet, so said Nan, amid loud laughter.

The actors, so pleased with their successful performance, never noticed Annabel's silence, and neither did Cousin Adelaide, who was laughing as much as anyone. Cries of " Wasn't it splendid ? But, oh, Nan, look at your dress, your hair, your face ! " came from everybody. Nettie was just as bad. Lady Annabel pretended she'd enjoyed it immensly. " Oh, isn't she a sport ? " they cried in ecstasy ; and how she ran. Mrs. Addington was brought to hear how the Indians chased the paleface, and she wanted to know what on earth they'd used to stain their faces. All the boys were copper colour.

Nan grinned, and Nettie said it was a secret. The girls hadn't tried it.

9

Scarlet blankets were worn with great effect. Rose's feather dusters had been undone and decorated their heads, tightly bound on with ribbon.

" Just wait till Rose catches you," warned Cousin Adelaide.

Bits of every coloured stuff had been sewn on to their skirts, and the pistols (made of wood), and the sticks painted to imitate blood-stained tomahawks, were wonderfully impressive at a distance.

Every one was so hot and thirsty and came into the house for lemonade and gingerbread, while Rose produced tea for anyone who wanted it.

The party might have gone on for hours had not Mrs. Yelverton arrived to call upon Lady Annabel and Mrs. Sinclair.

The boys and girls slipped away quietly: the overpowering grandeur of Mrs. Yelverton quelled the tumult.

Neither Lady Annabel nor Mrs. Sinclair smiled when Mrs. Yelverton invited them both to dine the next evening, adding, as an inducement, there'd be an eight-course dinner, with everything out of season.

The guests had no chance of refusing the invitation, because just before it was given they had announced their intention of doing nothing but sit on the shore and watch for mackerel—some of the great big horse-mackerel that Billy said did go by some nights.

The visitor had come to say something else, but was rather doubtful about it. Perhaps these grand ladies would snub her. How could *poor* Mrs. Addington be related to Mrs. Sinclair?

Mrs. Yelverton's complaint was that the day before Billy had covered her white granite front steps with gravel—thrown it on in heaps. The steps looked dreadful, and would somebody tell him he must not do it again? He really ought to be made to clean some of it off.

"What? Billy?" Mrs. Sinclair's air was disapproving.

"As if he cou'd, the dear lamb," remarked Annabel, easily.

Billy said he was sorry; of course he'd clean it up. He just loved sweeping. That was a terrible fierce butler Mrs. Yelverton had, and she couldn't tell him to take away that awful stuff; adding blandly that he hadn't meant to make the steps so dirty, but he and Tommy were building forts—it was such a nice place to do it. Having been in the house all day and not allowed to play Wild Indians, he would have done anything to get out, so ran off to consult Rose. If she sometimes said he was naughty no one else was allowed to, and she was furious that Mrs. Yelverton should be coming up here making out Billy was a bad boy, when Rose knew he was only what you'd call a *real boy*. And Tommy had just as much to do with it as Billy. Clean those steps? Why, Rose would do them—now, at once. They never were clean anyway, Rose knew that—her voice was loud— and other people knew it too before she'd finished talking. She hurriedly grabbed cleaning materials and rushed over to the Yelvertons', swept off the gravel, and washed every step till it shone.

Lil and Nan dashed after the whirlwind, but retreated on seeing what she was doing. When Rose had finished she rang the front door bell and informed the butler that he'd better take a good look. Those steps were clean—they'd never been before—and he might as well see to it that the lazy servants kept 'em like that.

Before he could suitably reply to these unpleasant truths—she was quite right—she departed, waving the bucket and the broom she brought down with her.

"That Mrs. Yelverton," explained Rose to Nan, "is frightened to death of most servants, but that hired man just gives her the black fits!"

Billy was ever so excited and waited, holding

Doll and Boarder, to see Cousin Adelaide and Lady Annabel dressed for the Yelvertons' dinner-party. Cousin looked very elegant—regal, Mrs. Addington said.

" Far, far away from the stars," commented Nan.

Mrs. Sinclair's dress had a little detached train, which Billy carried round as she moved about, and shook as if he were shaking mats for Rose, and Cousin never said " don't." She was wearing pearls—wonderful pearls, even Mrs. Yelverton had nothing like them ; but when Lady Annabel appeared they all sat up. She was one of the women who pay for dressing, and her maid had dressed her. She wore white and diamonds. Nan said she looked like a fairy, and Lil—very much impressed—remarked she was perfect, like her name, Lady Annabel.

There was something ethereal and wonderful about her, and Nan cried, "You're both fairies."

" Wearing starshine "—Billy pointed to the jewels.

" It's a shame your mother isn't coming," said Lady Annabel.

So it was, but they hadn't thought of that.

" Nobody axed me, sir, she said," laughed Mrs. Addington, who hadn't the slightest yearning to go and have dinner with the Yelvertons, and guessed pretty correctly—if she had been asked and possessed a dress to wear—the sort of reception they'd give her.

"Your mother would look best of all," asserted Annabel.

"Oh," sighed Nan, "I do wish mother was going too!"

"But I don't want to," protested Mrs. Addington.

"I'd rather stay here too." Annabel looked all round. "It's so comfortable, and I'm sure Rose has got something lovely for supper."

"She has. I went out to show her my dress," said Cousin.

"I did too." Lady Annabel smiled to herself.

"Why I'd be just crazy to go," Lil put in, quickly. "Don't you want to have all the beautiful things to eat and wear your jewels? They'll have on their grandest things. They pay an awful lot for them."

"Money isn't everything, Lil." Cousin Adelaide looked annoyed.

"I can't understand it at all," said Lil, puzzled. "We're so poor and we only have supper——"

"Rose is a splendid cook," protested Cousin Adelaide, and Lady Annabel murmured, "Marvellous!"

Lil continued breathless : " You're going to be waited on by lots of servants, and have everything to eat that costs heaps of money, and—and——"

" Things that cost heaps aren't always nicest," observed Lady Annabel. " For one thing, money doesn't make people pleasant."

" Well, I think it does," retorted Lil. " If Mummy had lots of money they'd all run after her."

" Mummy's an angel." Nan's arm went round her mother, and she glared defiantly at her sister. " Lil, you're crazy."

" Mummy's better'n any queen—so there ! " proclaimed Billy.

" The limousine's come," called Nan ; " it's a beauty, and doesn't look hired."

" May I sit outside and drive over there with you ? " begged Billy. " I'll run home quick's quick."

" The man can drive you back," said Cousin Adelaide.

" Oh, Cousin Adelaide, your cloak "—Lil was awestruck—" all feathers ; what a lovely thing ! So is Lady Annabel's. Be sure you remember to tell me all about the dinner and what they wear. Nettie's going to it. She has a splendid new dress for it ! "

CHAPTER X

" I'D LOVE TEN DOLLARS ! "

NAN's casual account of a derelict table up
in the loft did not interest anyone, and she
hadn't said much about it, for the memory of
that horrid day was painful. Feeling desperately
ashamed, she consigned that table to oblivion.

She was out fishing with Billy, and Cousin
Adelaide had come to steer. Tony Yelverton
was prowling about in his dinghy and rowed
over to them. He gazed at dishevelled Nan
putting bait on Billy's hook, and called :

" Say, Nan, Lil said you found a table up
in the loft of your barn. Let's see it."

The girl had no desire to be reminded of her
escape from the loft, so answered shortly, " I'll
show it to you some time."

" I guess Mother'll want to have a look at it
too. She might buy it. She's crazy about old
stuff. It's so fashionable now."

" 'Tisn't for sale," replied Nan ; and just
then Billy caught a fish.

"It's a Tommy cod, Cousin Adelaide—a real big one for your supper," rejoiced Billy, as Nan took it off the hook and killed it quickly.

"Hate to see the poor things flopping about," she explained.

Tony rowed off because he was afraid Billy might catch another fish and expect him to kill it. He was much too immaculately turned out for that, and, though he admired Mrs. Sinclair, didn't see why he should bother himself for a little boy, even if the Addingtons did have grand relations.

"I'd like to see that table too. Why don't you let us all inspect it?" demanded Cousin Adelaide, as the girl moored the boat and put the fish in a basket for Billy to take to Rose.

"All right," answered Nan.

It was a struggle to get her find down the ladder, but Wood helped her. Once down in the brighter light it was not a handsome object; caked dust and cobwebs were thick on it, and Rose—miraculously appearing out of the blue, sensing something happening—announced in her opinion it was old junk and no good to anyone.

Nan sadly agreed with her, but she needed a little table in her bedroom, and didn't see why she shouldn't have this one if she could get the dirt off. So she proceeded with the work, and Rose stood by with advice and dusters.

" I don't call it ugly," proclaimed Nan ; " it's looking nicer every minute. The top is frightfully scratched, but the edge is turned out like a shell. Look, Rose ! There are shells on the legs too."

" I'm not struck on it," replied Rose. " It's awful dark : may be dirt, but I think it's mahogany. You'll never get a shine on it. Some people might think it pretty. There are lots of queer folks everywhere."

It was hot work rubbing away at that piece of furniture, but it did look cleaner, though Nan feared Rose was right that it would take months to get any shine on it. But at least it wasn't dusty now.

If only she could get hold of Cousin Adelaide and find out what sort of a table she thought it was. But Cousin wasn't to be found, and then Nan decided to get Wood to carry the table up to the house. Lady Annabel might know something about such things.

" Hullo, Nan ! " There was Tony Yelverton. " Mother's in the barn, looking at your table."

Nan ran in. " Do you think it's ever going to look decent ? " she asked. " I've done verything I can but it won't polish yet."

Mrs. Yelverton, bending over the find, turned it round and straightened herself.

"I'll buy that table, Nan. I can't say I think much of it, but that old furniture is all the go now, and it might do for a room in my New York house."

"Rose thinks it's made of mahogany," said Nan, "but it's not for sale. You know it's not mine—it belongs to Mother, and I couldn't do anything without telling her first. I'm going to put it in my bedroom." She pushed the table away. "I'm sorry you can't have it if you want it, but I told Tony it wasn't for sale."

"Here's ten dollars." Mrs. Yelverton pressed two five dollar bills into the girl's hand; they fell on the floor, and in sheer amazement Nan picked them up, but handed them back.

Mrs. Yelverton waved fat hands in protest. "Ten dollars, Nan, will buy you a great deal which you need. Even with such grand relations 't seems to me you don't get many new lothes." Her voice was contemptuous. Nan clenched her hands. "Get the man to come ⸱ for it, Tony. I've got the carriage out in he road," she explained. "It's heavy, and ony couldn't carry it."

"No, you don't, Tony." Nan's eyes were

blazing, and she seated herself on top of the table, which cracked ominously.

" Be careful, you'll break it," said Mrs. Yelverton, sharply. " Here, take the money."

" It's Mother's table and I'm not going to sell it, so there—not for fifty dollars."

Mrs. Yelverton laughed. " Oh, but you'd never get fifty dollars for that old thing. Ten's too much, but I wouldn't be mean. I'm sure I'm making you a splendid offer—generous too. Fifty dollars ! Why——" Mrs. Yelverton seemed quite shocked by that idea. " Tony, go and get the man."

" Tony won't do anything of the sort "—the now thoroughly roused Nan was indignant. " Mrs. Yelverton, I really and truly cannot do what you want, though I'd love to, ever so. It's not mine, and Mother mightn't like it ; " and only Nan knew how much she longed to get the ten dollars just waiting to be taken. Why she could buy—what couldn't she buy with it ? There were so many things she needed.

" I'm going to have it." Nan glanced up in astonishment. Mrs. Yelverton had come nearer, and in the rather dim light of the barn seemed altered. Her face looked—why she looked almost cruel. And there was a queer glint in her eyes. It wasn't difficult to imagine her

being dreadfully rough. It was all so strange.
It was—well, not frightening ; who could be
frightened of fat, harmless Mrs. Yelverton ?
Her eyes looked so queer and she came so close,
as if she was going to grab the table.

" You're not going to take it, are you ? "
laughed Nan.

" Ten dollars will be of much more use to you
than a ridiculous table," returned Mrs. Yelverton,
crossly. " And, anyway, I don't believe it's
made of anything good like mahogany. I like
the shape of it. You are silly not to jump at
the chance of getting so much money. Tony,
get that table out at once. Nan, here's the
money ; " again she pressed the bills into Nan's
hand. " I'm not going to wait any longer ; "
but again Nan returned the bills.

" You'll have to go and ask Mother if you
want to buy it," said the girl, with
determination.

" I know your mother would be delighted,
and we're only wasting time," replied Mrs.
Yelverton, " so I shall take it."

" You shan't !—you shan't ! " retorted Nan,
shrilly.

" Why, I'm giving you a perfectly splendid
price, and you know it. You have a very rude
way of treating a customer. I buy a very

great deal from your mother, and I always pay
the highest prices."

" Too high, I guess," said Tony.

" What is happening ? " said Cousin Adelaide.

Nan wasn't surprised, for she had heard foot-
steps, and through the crack of the door had seen
the glint of Cousin Adelaide's white dress long before its wearer arrived.   The Yelvertons gasped.
Tony pushed his mother away and said, " We're
just making a little visit to see the table."

Time to collect herself was what Mrs.
Yelverton wanted, and Tony gave it to her.
The nasty, shifty look left her face, and she
explained with a beaming smile that she pro-
posed to buy an old table that Nan had found
in the loft. She had come specially to see it. She
was certain that Mrs. Sinclair would be sensible
about it. Why, actually, Nan declined to part
with it. So ridiculous !

" But, cousin, I can't ; it's Mother's, and
I've said it over and over again," protested Nan.
" How can I sell it when she doesn't know one
thing about it ? Mrs. Yelverton says Tony's
to get her man to take it away now—that's why
I'm sitting on it—and she'll give me ten dollars.
I'd love ten dollars," added candid Nan, " but
I can't take it. If only Mrs. Yelverton would
go and ask Mother."

Cousin Adelaide's gaze was icy as she contemplated the Yelvertons with a long, slow look. Her silence too was impressive. Tony promptly and unobtrusively got out of the barn. He found Mrs. Sinclair's penetrating eyes disconcerting. Nan slipped off the table, and Mrs. Yelverton said :

"Do look at it, Mrs. Sinclair. You'll say ten dollars is a good price. It's only rubbish, but I've a fancy for a table like that. I have one in my boudoir in New York, and I want another to match it. Of course it'll cost something to have it French polished. Nan needs the money, I know. Ten dollars is a great deal for a girl and——"

Mrs. Sinclair interrupted her.

"Nan can't sell that table, it's her mother's. She's told you so. If you want to buy it, go and see Mrs. Addington. Wood!" called the determined Cousin.

"Yes'm, coming," and he appeared at the door.

"Just take that table up to the house and give it to Rose." There was silence while Wood removed it. "I think it's a particularly good table. I believe if it were sent to New York it would be worth much more than ten dollars. We can have it valued if you like. Oh, you're going! You won't ask Mrs. Addington ? Good-

bye," and, with a casual nod, Cousin stood while
the dejected Mrs. Yelverton made a ponderous
way out by the back gate. Cousin watched
her shut it and went back to Nan. They sank
down on a heap of hay.

"Nan, that woman! Why, I'm beginning
to think that ancient piece of furniture is some
good."

"She was sort of queer," observed Nan. "I
would have loved ten dollars. Didn't it seem
funny to you—— Mrs. Yelverton was so
different and made a fuss."

"Cross, I suppose," stated Cousin Adelaide,
who had no intention of airing her candid
opinion of the incident. "I don't know much
about furniture, but I think Mrs. Yelverton does.
I wonder if your mother would let me send the
table to a dealer in New York? He's honest,
I know."

"Of course she would. I don't like Mrs.
Yelverton."

"You stopped her getting a bargain; I
suppose that ruffled her." Cousin Adelaide's
voice was careless, but for all she seemed calm,
inwardly she was raging. How dared those two
treat Nan that way? She'd heard Tony's
remark about the prices. Why, they were
horrible, dreadful—just bullies to defenceless

Nan. And ten dollars—ten dollars for that!
Oh, how much she regretted having dined at
the Yelvertons'. If only she hadn't accepted
anything from them nor let Annabel. " Does
Lil like the Yelvertons very much ? "

" They have nice parties," explained Nan.

" I suppose it is dull for her here," murmured
Cousin, lost in thought.

" You'll never guess how thankful I was to
see you, Cousin. I felt—I felt——" Not for
worlds would Nan have acknowledged she was
almost frightened by the persistent Yelvertons.
She felt puzzled. " I thought I'd never get rid
of them. They didn't mind a word I said."

" Come, we'll go and find out your mother's
opinion. They thought you'd give in if they
kept on at you. They knew it was worth more
than ten dollars—ten dollars ! " added Mrs.
Sinclair, contemptuously. " Who's that ? "

It was Tony. He stood halfway in and
remarked, " I'll tell you something, Nan. I
saw you go up to the loft and I pulled away the
ladder. Ha ha ! Clever Nan ! "

The girl turned furiously. She grew scarlet,
her voice was shrill. " It was perfectly horrid
of you not to come back and put it up. Why,
I might have had to stay there all night,
and——"

10

" I think, without meaning to, you did Nan a good turn," said Cousin Adelaide, quietly. " If she hadn't been—well—marooned in the loft by you "—and her laugh made Nan feel less prickly and angry—" she wouldn't have discovered the table, and from the anxiety your mother showed for its possession I think it may be worth quite a lot." Tony vanished, and she took the girl's hand. " Dear Nan, you were splendid ! "

" I wanted to hit him ! " said the girl.

" Well, you didn't say so, did you ? "

Lady Annabel was leaving by the afternoon train, and Nan was making sandwiches for her and preparing a lunch basket.

" Let's put in a few olives," said Nan ; " she loves them. Lil, stop looking on and skin those sardines. I'll make them into a paste, which will be much easier to spread."

" You're making too much fuss," grumbled Lil. " What's the good ? There are plenty of cream cheese sandwiches—more than enough—and Rose is going to fill the thermos with coffee. I'm glad Lady Annabel is going. Yes, I am—so there."

" Well, I'm not. She's been most awfully kind, and wasn't it beautiful of her to give me that lovely gardening suit ? " demanded Nan.

" I feel like Robin Hood in it. It's so stylish,
I think."

" Oh, I know it's nice ; but she's always
talking about the Yelvertons, and I know she
disapproves of them," sighed Lil.

" So does Cousin."

" Yes, but she doesn't say so—anyway not
so often. I'm always afraid Mother will tell
me I can't go over there so much. And it's the
only place I ever do go to where there's any fun.
Was Mrs. Yelverton dreadfully nasty about the
table ? "

" Yes, she was horrid—she was so queer."

" I wish you'd let her buy it, Mother wouldn't
have minded," said Lil.

" Why, Lil Addington, are you crazy ? Then
we wouldn't have had the hundred dollars Lady
Annabel paid for it. Besides, if she gets more
for it in New York she's going to send it to
Mother. And we're going to get five dollars
each—now. What'll you do with your s ? I
think I'll have a new hat, and——"

" I will too," interrupted Lil ; " and I
hope you'll throw away that old scarecrow
thing you're so fond of ; it's a perfect dis-
grace."

" Lady Annabel says it's a lovely country
hat, just the right thing." Nan was quick in

defence of her adored hat.   "And I've just put a fresh trimming on it."

"It looks just what you paid for it—five cents ; anyone could tell that," replied Lil, scornfully.   "Do you know what Mother's going to do with the rest of that hundred dollars ? "

"Have the hall stove mended.   It'll take all that, and we'll be warm next winter.   Mother's been worrying dreadfully about it, for she didn't see how she could pay for it.   Oh, that blessed table, three cheers for it ! " laughed Nan.

"Nan, did you see how I altered my best dress ? " Lil almost whispered.

"No.   What for ?   When did you do it ? "

"The night I went to Tony's party at the hotel ; and, oh, Nan ! it was the night Lady Annabel arrived and Cousin Adelaide drove me home.   Lady Annabel saw my dress, the way I'd remade it, you know, but of course she didn't know I'd altered it, and she said it was fierce ! "

"She didn't," contradicted Nan.   "You know she'd never say that."

"Well, no, not exactly ; but she said it looked so grown-up and ugly without sleeves——"

"But there were sleeves."

" Yes, I know. Oh, hurry up ! You're so long over that lunch. I want to show you what I did to my dress."

" Why didn't you show it to me before ? "

" Well, you were out that day. And since then I haven't had a chance. I don't want anyone else to know, either."

" I'll come as soon as I've finished this. You wouldn't want me to do the lunch up anyhow, would you ? She's been so kind ; and look at the lovely Water Baby book she gave Billy, and those stockings of yours. They're solid silk too."

" I know they are. I'm a pig, but I hate being interfered with. They treat me as if I were so young. And I made my dress look lovely. I cut out the sleeves, and it's just like the pictures you see in ' Vogue.' The arms are bare and——"

" You never cut up that lovely dress Cousin had made for you ? "

" Yes, I did. Listen, Nan——"

" Why, it'll be ruined. How could you ? "

" It was a nasty old-fashioned-looking thing, a hundred years old. I couldn't bear wearing it. And Nettie says the way I've got it looks so fashionable. I've white arms, and every one's wearing dresses like that."

"It seems a dreadful waste," observed Nan. "And you know your arms are so thin. I thought that dress was so pretty, and you looked different somehow in it. Cousin Adelaide said it was so distinguished."

"Did she?" Lil began to wonder if those alterations of hers were silly. "Cousin Adelaide said that? But, oh, Nan! can't you see how I hate being just a little girl in a little girl's dress, and——"

"Does Mother know?" Lil shook her head. "Nor Cousin?"

"No; that is, I'm not sure about Cousin Adelaide. Perhaps she didn't notice that night. Anyhow, Lady Annabel talked about it, and Cousin didn't say anything then; but she may have seen the difference."

"Aren't you going to tell her?"

"No, I'm not. Do you think I ought to?"

"Well, I would," said Nan.

"Oh, botheration! I suppose I'll have to tell mother. She doesn't want me to look like Nettie's friends, and she won't like it."

"Well, I'm not struck on them myself," returned Nan, calmly, "but I like Nettie. Now if I could do dressmaking I'd put back the sleeves; there may be some use in learning it after all. Hurry up with those slices of bread

and butter. Oh, you've cut them much too
thick ! "

Lil cut some more.

" Here, let me," and Nan grabbed the loaf.

" I wonder why Cousin Adelaide doesn't hire
a motor and have it every day, not only when
Lady Annabel's here," said Lil.

" I'm sure we are all having a perfectly
beautiful time."

" Yes "—Lil spoke doubtfully—" but it's so
quiet. And I like the Yelverton's. They do
give me some fun. It's dreadfully dreary only
thinking about next year's strawberry plants.
But now I suppose Mrs. Yelverton won't ask
me there often. Lady Annabel wouldn't go to
the farewell party they gave for her, not even
after I told her they'd put it in the paper that
she was coming to it, and that they were having
it specially for her. She told Mrs. Yelverton
that she hadn't one free evening—not one. Of
course that notice in the paper and Lady
Annabel not being there did make the Yelvertons
feel so *small*. Every one expected to meet Lady
Annabel, and it was dreadfully awkward. Mrs.
Yelverton's very angry ; and you wouldn't
sell her the table, so that makes it worse."

" Oh, bother Mrs. Yelverton ! " said Nan,
impatiently. " Come on, let's get ready. I am

glad we're all going in the motor to the junction, and that Lady Annabel decided not to take the train from here. I do love a motor. Oh, but I wish she wasn't going at all!" Nan finished the basket with some little doylies and shouted for Billy to get his face washed.

The car was big, but it was a squeeze with all the baggage and bundles. There were shrieks of joy from Billy—even parting from Doll and Boarder hadn't depressed him. He knew there was no room for them on this trip. Every one except Lil was sorry to say good-bye to Lady Annabel.

They waved and waved to her as the big train moved slowly and majestically out of the junction. Billy was entranced. There were so many trains shunting, and such beautiful big engines. Oh, and a red one just like his!

" I'd love to live near these trains," he sighed. " We've only got such nasty little ones at home. Cousin, I think I'll be an engine-driver when I'm big."

" What about that candy store ? " asked his mother.

" One freight train has hundreds and hundreds of 'mense cars ; I've counted them," cried the little boy, joyfully.

Then Cousin Adelaide explained she had a

surprise for them. She had brought lunch with her. The others hadn't even thought of that. They got into the car and Cousin told the driver to go back till he saw a nice place to stop. He pulled up by a brook all ripples and brown water. They chose a place where the grass was short and shaded by beech trees, and the girls carried cushions and rugs and made seats for Mother and Cousin Adelaide, so that they could lean back against the tree trunks.

"What a heavenly spot! Who thought of this joyful thing?" asked Mrs. Addington.

"I did," answered Cousin Adelaide. "I hid the baskets and got everything from the Woman's Exchange."

"And now, mummy, you and cousin are not allowed to do anything at all," ordered Nan. She was shown how to manage the spirit lamp, and there was water in bottles to fill the kettle. "I wish Lady Annabel could have stayed longer; but it's scrumptitious, Cousin Adelaide, that you didn't have to go too."

"She had a lovely time," remarked Mrs. Sinclair, "and told me to be sure and make you all understand how very happy she had been."

Lil shook her head. She couldn't believe that. Dull, dreary place, she called it, but kept this to herself.

"I'd like to give a picnic—all my own," said Billy. "I'd have it for Rose. She hasn't been to one. She's always getting things ready for us, and she has a new dress for the church social ; but I can't have a picnic, for I haven't any money."

"Don't fish," reproved Lil.

"Not fishin'. I had forty cents once, but it's spent." No one inquired how he obtained that money, and only Nan knew, but she didn't say anything. "Tommy would buy my red aigine, but I don't want him to, and——"

"Of course not," interrupted Cousin Adelaide. "I don't see why you shouldn't give Rose a picnic."

"With the tea basket ? It's a lovely kettle."

"Don't bother, Cousin Adelaide," said Nan.

"It wouldn't be a dreadful, horrid bother like doing lessons, would it ? " demanded Billy, earnestly ; and on being assured there'd be nothing like lessons about it, jumped up. "I'll go and talk to that man that drives the car. I guess I'll be a motor-man and——" He stopped. "Where's the car ? "

Nan and Lil exclaimed at the same moment : "The car ! It isn't there ! "

"Wait," said Cousin Adelaide, "wait ! "

"Listen." Billy ran down to the road; there was the motor and out of it got Rose. "Oh, Mrs. Sinclair!" she gasped, "I thought he'd never come for me. And when he did come—my! but he's nearly killed me driving so fast. Oh, Billy, isn't it lovely? It's a surprise!" Rose, voluble and delighted, was given a cushion and loudly welcomed. "Wasn't it just lovely of Mrs. Sinclair? She planned it. Fifty times I've nearly let it out. But that driver—I warned him. I said, 'Young man, you'll die early. You'll get into a grave faster'n you know. You're drivin' straight to it.' But he didn't mind me. Coffee?" as Nan gave her a cup. "If it don't beat all!"

"It's just splendid, Rose, that you came." Billy threw himself down beside her. "I was just talking about you, and I wanted to give you a picnic, and here you are having one."

"Mrs. Sinclair wouldn't let me make a thing," cried Rose. "She bought it all. I am hungry, and motor ridin' is fine. But I did wish he'd go slow, so that all the folks could see me."

"You'd have been late if he had, and got cold coffee," answered Lil.

"It's a lovely place, this," said Rose. "I wouldn't wonder if there were bears in these woods. My mother remembers a man killing

one out here once when she was a little
girl."

"Oh!" Billy's eyes shone; "did she ever
see a bear?"

"I dunno as she did," replied Rose, "but
she heard that the men were going out after
'em. They took sheep. The woods was all
thick then. My that's good coffee, never
tasted better!" which was praise indeed.

"Mary, I have an invitation from Mrs. Perry
Earlwood to go over for dinner to-morrow and
stay all night. She's at the cottage at Bear
Cove, and has some nice young people staying
there. She'd love to have Lil come too. What
do you say?"

"That would be charming." Mrs. Addington
turned to Lil: "Do you want to go?"

"Oh, mummy, I'd adore it," replied Lil,
eagerly.

"We'll drive over in the limousine, and, Lil,
I'll lend you a suitcase," said Cousin Adelaide.
"All you need to take will pack into it. I've
got some blue slippers and a dressing-gown to
match, and you can have them if you like."

"Oh, thank you, it will be lovely!" said
Lil; "but——" She- stopped. "Cousin
Adelaide, what shall I take to wear in the
evening?"

" Your white *crêpe de Chine,*" replied Mrs. Sinclair.

" But I cut the sleeves out of it, and—and——" stammered the embarrassed girl, " it's got no sleeves at all. I did it the night of Tony's party, because I wanted to look grown-up like the others. I made the neck low too."

" Why, Lil, you must have spoiled it," said her mother gravely.

Lil blushed and looked dreadfully worried. " It isn't spoiled "—she hesitated—" it's different."

" I'm afraid it wouldn't be suitable to wear at a quiet little dinner "—Cousin Adelaide spoke kindly. " When we go home you can drive down to the dressmaker's and take the dress. She can put in something in the way of lace and chiffon. You can't wear a ball dress at a country cottage. I'll come to the dressmaker with you. It must be done at once."

" Oh, Cousin Adelaide, you are good ! I was afraid you'd be dreadfully cross with me," and Lil's depression vanished, and Nan whistled.

CHAPTER XI

THEATRICALS

NAN and Nettie Yelverton sat on the stile between the two houses, eating apples. It was a low and comfortable stile, most suitable for sitting on, and made a short cut from Nan's to Nettie's. A whitewashed picket fence stretched on each side of it, which proud eminence was known as the "Elevated Railway," and much used by Billy and Tommy as a route to the shore. Nan gazed at it as she threw away the core of her apple.

"Let's walk down the 'elevated' and see what the boys are doing in the boathouse," she suggested, with a reckless disregard of consequences, since she invariably tore her skirt on the pickets.

Nettie shook her head.

"No. You said you'd ask your mother if you could act in my theatricals, and you never have. I want to know to-day."

"I—half forgot," carelessly. "You can't

have theatricals now, Nettie. Vacation's nearly
over, and the boys are going away. I wish they
weren't. What do you want me to do,
anyway ? "

Nettie pulled a copy of a play from her
pocket.

" Your part is dancing. This is where you
come in : *Appearance of the Fairy.* That would
be you, and now listen. You'll have to wear a
soft satin dress, not too long—you must show
your feet. It will have to be scarlet, and you
must get Professor Dupré at the dancing class
to show you how to do the dance. You can
easily do that."

" I can't ! He won't be back till October—
he can't teach me any dance when he isn't here."

" I never meant him to, silly ! The play's
not till the Christmas vacation ; we're coming
back for part of it. It's the fashion "
—patronizingly—" to spend Christmas in the
country now."

" Look here "—Nan had a qualm—" will it
be very expensive for that dress ? "

" Goodness, no "—carelessly. " Oh, Nan,
you'll look stunning with a wreath in your hair,
all diamond spangles ! See, here's the sketch."

She held out a coloured picture, at which both
girls gazed with rapture.

"Isn't the skirt rather short?" Nan demanded.

"No! You simply couldn't have it any longer—to really dance."

"Slippers to match the skirt! Aren't they *ducky*?"

"The stockings match too." Nettie pointed to them. "Aren't they sweet? You'll have to send to New York for them and the slippers."

Nan's qualm deepened into plain misgiving. Scarlet satin shoes did not arrive without money, even if you "sent to New York." She could dance almost anything, and she knew it, or Nettie would never have asked her. And to wear those slippers, and that dress, and dance just once in them!

"Oh, I've simply got to do it," she burst out, for there must be *some* way she could get hem. "Only I'm certain Mother will say I can't!"

"Don't ask her," Nettie advised, casually. "Just say you're going to do it; that's the way I manage. And come over to our house and tell me what she says. Hurry!"

Mrs. Addington was alone when her younger daughter bounced in on her with a torn stocking, from an injudicious return by the "elevated railway," and a scarlet picture in her hand.

"Mummy, I've promised Nettie to dance in

her theatricals at Christmas," she flung out like a bomb. "Look, here's the sketch of the dress I'm to wear—and I'll have to get five or six dancing lessons from Professor Dupré. Won't it be lovely ? "

Her mother gazed dumbly at the picture.

" Isn't it dear ?" Nan cried, fervently. " Look at the slippers and the stockings—just like the skirt ! Nettie says we can easily get them from New York."

" Oh, Nan, I know." Mrs. Addington put her hand to her forehead. " Only, I'm afraid —we can't manage it."

" Oh, mother "—blankly.

" It would be all very well for Nettie, but how on earth do you think you could get the money to pay for a dress with yards of satin in it ? "

" There are my blackberries," Nan reminded her weakly. " They'll bring in a lot, and they're almost ripe."

" But they were to buy your winter dress, dear. You must have a warm suit. And the money for them wouldn't begin to pay for this dress, and Professor Dupré's dancing lessons."

" Then——" Nan caught her breath and stopped. " Mother," she said, desperately, " there are Cousin Adelaide's dressmaking lessons. I never told you, but I don't *want*

11

them. I just hate dressmaking, and Cousin
Adelaide never even asked me what I wanted;
she just took it from Lil. If she'd give me the
money for a nest-egg for college, or something
I wanted—but I feel as if I'd just die if I had
to go and learn how to sew seams. Can't I go
and tell her so? And say, if she doesn't like
girls going to college—and you know she
doesn't—could I take the old dressmaking
money and have the only thing I ever wanted
so dreadfully badly in all my life ? "

" You can ask her "—doubtfully. " Only,
Nan——"

But Nan had rushed upstairs and into Cousin
Adelaide's room. In ten minutes she returned.

" Cousin says no," she said, morosely. " She
wouldn't even listen about college, and she says
every girl should have dressmaking lessons, and
they'll do me far more good than dancing in
Nettie Yelverton's silly play. At least that's
what she meant—she didn't say it like that."

" Nan, dear. I think you'll have to refuse,"
her mother said, gently.

" Oh, mummy, I can't ! Can't I find some
way to do it ? Nettie says I'd look distracting
in that dress with a diamond wreath in my hair.
And you know my feet are nice, and I'd love
those red shoes ! "

"I do know, Nan, but I don't see how you can have the things," her mother reiterated, in desperation. "I can't give you the money for them; you might as well ask for the moon. You'll see it yourself if you think it over!"

Nan stamped her foot. "It's just because it's *me*!" she burst out, recklessly. "If Lil wanted anything she'd get it, but *I* never can have what I want—never! I think you and Cousin Adelaide might have done something, and everything's just perfectly horrid, and I hate it all!"

She flung herself out of the room, too angry to listen to reason. Mrs. Addington put her hand up to her head, which generally ached all day if no one but Rose had noticed it, and went on with her sewing. She had never seen good, loyal Nan in such a temper, and knew perfectly well the girl would soon be sorry for it; but in the meantime there was no sense in going after her : she was best alone ; but all the same Mrs. Addington sighed, as Cousin Adelaide sailed down, rather ruffled.

"Was Nan here?" she asked. "I hope, Mary, you didn't really want her to give up those dressmaking lessons and squander the money on some finery for Nettie Yelverton's

play ?   I thought it would be extremely foolish,
and I told Nan so."

" She is so dreadfully disappointed," Mrs.
Addington said, wearily.' " Oh, I told her, too,
that it was quite impossible.   It is not like Nan
either, to want such frivolities.   She'll probably
be here in a minute to tell you she was silly."

But dinner time arrived and no Nan.   Lil
knew better than to look in their room for her;
Nan had haunts of her own when things went
wrong ; but even Lil had no idea where Nan
had taken her rage and despair.

Back of the Addingtons' house was a deserted
road which the village people had used for a
short-cut across the fields to the Yelvertons',
till Mrs. Yelverton had had a stout rail fence
built across the end of it.   No one haunted the
old road now but Nan, who loved the wild lilies
and thick wild pear that grew along the sides
of it, and the ferns that filled the old tracks in
the middle.   And in the ferns she lay now, flat
on her face, Nettie's picture of the red-skirted
dancer clutched in one outstretched hand, and
the tear in her stocking displayed to the greatest
advantage.   For the rest she was a dishevelled
heap of blue cotton frock, and a mop of untidy
brown curls, prone in the green fern.

It was thus that a much-astounded gentleman

beheld her, and brought to a full stop the protesting Cadillac he had been obstinately endeavouring to navigate over what had long been anything but a road.

"Well," said Mr. Perry Earlwood, blankly. But Nan was as dead to his voice as she had been to the purr of his car. She lay in the road and sobbed in sheer abandon. Mr. Perry Earlwood sat in his car, which was up to its mud guards in ferns, and considered her. Something about the curly brown head combined with a blue cotton frock seemed familiar to him, and suddenly he remembered the girl who had stood on the bank, at the Yelvertons' picnic, when a small boy rowed him in to shore.

"Mary Addington's girl," he observed, to himself this time. "Just as well I did get stuck, or I'd have been over her. Now, I wonder——" But he did not say what. Instead he descended heavily from his car, honked his motor-horn, and stood with his back turned to the blue cotton heap while he lit a cigar. When he turned back again Miss Nan Addington sat bolt upright staring at him.

"How d'ye do?" inquired Mr. Earlwood. If he observed Nan's swollen eyes and tear-blotched face he did not mention them.

"I don't do at all," said Nan, recklessly, and

gulped. " I'm perfectly *miserable* ! And if it
were Lil who wanted anything silly Cousin
Adelaide would just give it to her, but she won't
do one single thing I want. She knows I'm
dying to go to college, and she won't help me,
and she won't let me dance in Nettie Yelverton's
theatricals because it's a waste of the money
she gave me for dressmaking lessons. I—I
simply couldn't live through dressmaking
lessons. I "—she caught herself up in the
middle of a sob—" I don't see what you're doing
here. This isn't a road."

" It's marked as one on the map," Mr.
Earlwood responded, blandly. " But I agree
with you that it doesn't seem to be one. As
for what I'm doing here, I'm rather interested
in this country." Could Nan only have known
what the casual words would have meant to the
dying rail-road that linked Happy Valley with
civilization !—"And I just called in on my way
to town to take Johnston and the Allen boys
for a bit of a jaunt. But as this road doesn't
seem to be getting me to them, suppose you
and I have one instead. Will your mother be
worrying about you ?

Nan shook her head.

" Then suppose we have lunch," said Mr.
Earlwood.

" But the boys ? " gasped Nan.

" Blessed are they who expect nothing—the boys don't know I'm coming. Is that water clean ? " with a sudden glance at the brook on one side of the road.

Nan was abruptly aware of a swollen face and scarlet eyes ; also, with a furious blush, of her torn stocking.

" Quite clean," she returned, confusedly. " I'll be back in a moment.

" Well, don't drink any." Mr. Earlwood was an expert in water.

It was a very sleek and shamefaced Nan who returned in five minutes to gaze thunderstruck. Mr. Earlwood had a table across his car, with various items of the boys' lunch spread on it. But his whole attention was bestowed on Nettie's sketch of the red dancing dress, which the startled Nan had left behind her.

" Help yourself to coffee," said he, pointing to a thermos bottle, " and pour me out some ; and, if you don't mind, now that we seem to be more composed, would you tell me what all your Niobe disguise is about ? "

" I never should have said anything "— helplessly. But Nan caught Mr. Earlwood's calmly pitiless eye, and told the whole story.

" H—m," said he. " Have another sandwich. Was it this thing you wanted to look like—instead of having dressmaking lessons ? "

" Why not ? " said Nan, bluntly.

" Because it's *démodé* "—Mr. Earlwood rose to the occasion recklessly. " If you'd had even one of those despised dressmaking lessons you'd know it's *d-é-m-o-d-é*, out of fashion ! Nobody dances in a thing like that now. I'd scrap that, with young Miss Yelverton's theatricals. Now, what else was it you murmured about books and college ? "

" I want to go to it—I mean college." There was something terribly truth-compelling about Mr. Earlwood or his sandwiches. " And if I had all the new books about strawberry farming I might be able to make the money to get there. Mother and Wood are just—just conventicle ! "

The stout Mr. Earlwood threw back his head and laughed. " I don't know that it isn't a perfectly good word, all the same," he explained, " but d'ye know what I think is *your* course of action ? Just wait, and get hold of those farming books somewhere. I believe I've some I could send you ; go and tell Miss Nettie you're not taking any of her dancing stunts, and *go on* with those dressmaking lessons. I never saw a girl who needed 'em worse ; that dress you have on sags behind now ! "

Nan burst out into real and joyful laughter, but Mr. Earlwood was quite grave.

" Half the way to a cultivated mind is a cultivated appearance," said he, firmly, " and we'll begin with those lessons right now. Here " —he burrowed in an inside pocket and dug out a case of thread and a needle—" you sew up that landslide in your stocking, and you and I'll go and call on Nettie Yelverton. The car'll be all right here—fact, I don't know how it's ever to be got out of this ! "

" I don't know how I'm ever to tell Nettie I can't afford it," Nan blurted.

" You don't have to ; I never give a reason when I get out of a deal I can't afford. I'm just done with it." Mr. Earlwood heaved himself to his feet. " Come along."

Nettie Yelverton was entertaining some girl friends on the lawn as Nan and Mr. Earlwood arrived. Nan gasped, and would have run ; but Mr. Earlwood had command of the situation.

" Miss Nan has something private to say to you, Miss Nettie. No, don't call your mother out ; this isn't a call." He turned his back as Nan said shakily that she couldn't dance, that was all. But his somewhat large ears took in Nettie's answer.

" Mother said you wouldn't be able to.

" Of course your mother couldn't give you your dress, but I thought the Honourable Mrs. Sinclair might have ; she gave Lil hers for our party. Mother says it must be humiliating to be so poor. But I'd just as soon give your part to somebody else.

" All right," said Nan, shakily, and turned away. It was as well Nettie could not see her face, for tears were running down it.

Mr. Perry Earlwood said nothing, good or bad, but as they reached the shelter of the first trees a large and comforting hand enveloped Nan's.

" You get along home, my little lady," he observed, with some significance. " Tell your mother you've been lunching with me, and I feel seventy years younger. Good-bye."

But as Nan disappeared Mr. Earlwood stood lost in thought.

" Never dreamt Mary Addington was in such deep water," he muttered, and suddenly laughed out. " By George, I'd better get an expert to pick out those books on strawberry farming while Miss Nan's waiting to go to college ! "

There was no joke as far as the empty road could see, but Mr. Perry Earlwood chuckled all the way back to his car.

CHAPTER XII

THE GOLD THREAD

IT was four o'clock, and there was no sign of Nan.

Cousin Adelaide, to her astonishment, felt the house dreary without Nan's laugh in it, and took refuge on the veranda and the society of Billy. He had been sitting there quietly, wonderful to relate, for half an hour, with a book in his hand and his nose screwed up in deep concentration. Cousin Adelaide leaned over suddenly and smoothed his soft yellow chrysanthemum head.

"Oh!" said Billy, detachedly. "I'm learning my lesson: school begins to-morrow. Could you hear me say it?"

Cousin Adelaide gazed at the book he handed her. "Are you learning poetry, Billy?" she inquired, absently.

"No; it's a brave hymn," Billy retorted, scornfully.

"What in the world is a brave hymn?"

" That "—he put a grubby forefinger on his book. " Now you hear me say it :

' They have come from tribulation
    And have washed their robes in blood.
Washed them in the Blood of Jesus ;
    Tried they were and firm they stood.
Mocked, imprisoned, stoned, tormented,
    Sawn asunder, slain with sword,
They have conquered death and Satan,
    By the might of Christ their Lord.' "

" Well, it is a brave hymn," Cousin Adelaide agreed.

" Must have been awful, musn't it ? " Billy commented, cheerfully. " We're going to have Johnnycake for tea, Cousin. Wouldn't you like me to read you the story of the Palace of the King, to pass the time till it's ready ? You know where the Palace is ? "

" No, I'm afraid I don't," Cousin Adelaide returned, meekly.

" Well, you wait till I get the book.' " He dived into the house and returned with a slim volume. " The name of it's really ' The Gold Thread,' " he announced, importantly, " but this is how it begins : ' Once upon a time a boy named Eric lost his way in a vast forest. He was the son of the good King Magnus . . . ' "

and on and on went the piping little voice in the story of the boy whose father had given him a gold thread to guide him, and who threw it away to run after all sorts of strange things. How he met the swineherd Wolf, and was taken to the robbers' castle ; how he was set free by the boy he had befriended, and was hunted with bloodhounds by the robber captain ; how he was not harmed by them and got back his gold thread, which led him past a lion in safety, and at last guided him home. " ' Then,' " Billy finished, with triumph, " ' the sun set and the earth was dark, and the Palace of the King shone like an aurora in the wintry sky.' "

" It's not always easy to hold on to the gold thread," Cousin Adelaide soliloquized, wondering suddenly where Nan was.

" You just have to go right along, and try and remember what's right," Billy explained. " You see the sky up there between the pine-trees, Cousin ? Well, that's the road to the moon, and that big white way you see lighted up there at night, that's the track to the Palace of the King. I've known that ever since I was really a little boy. Did you like the story ? "

" Loved it "—truthfully. " How well you read, Billy ! "

" Oh, I didn't 'zactly read it," Billy confessed calmly. " I know it most by heart."

" But you turned over the leaves ! "

" To get to the pictures." Billy yawned. " I'm awfully hungry."

" Who told you about the road to the moon, and the white way to the King's Palace ? " questioned Cousin Adelaide, curiously.

" Oh, I thought of it when I was little, and Mummy thinks it looks the right way. Of course "—with conviction—" Mummy never lets the gold thread go : she's bound to get to the King's Palace. I don't want her to get there before me though ; I'd be a lonely boy without her."

" Billy, your tea's ready," Rose interrupted from the side door, and glanced at the book on his lap. " Land sakes, Mrs. Sinclair, if he ain't been telling you about his King's Palace ! It used to worry me, but he and Tommy Yelverton were as bad as they could be this morning, and I guess he ain't sickening for anything yet."

She let the door bang and disappeared. Billy slid off his chair.

" All the people in the brave hymn must have had a gold thread, musn't they ? " he demanded, unexpectedly. " 'Spect it's easier for grown-

up people. I was fearful bad yesterday, and
Mrs. Yelverton's coming up to tell Mummy,"
with engaging frankness. "We were just
doing an errand in the village, and errands are
much duller since I promised Mummy I wouldn't
ring all the door-bells and then run away, and
Mrs. Yelverton came along in her carriage. She
has the *fattest* coachman, Cousin Adelaide"—
with sudden ease—"much fatter than Mr.
Yelverton. And her horses are so tied up with
check-reins they can't go fast, they only look
fast. So Tommy and I chased her, and yelled
loud at her, and she threw us ten cents to go
away. Ten cents to go away was fine, so we
did it again this morning. But she's coming to
tell Mummy about me, and—I only feel sort of
empty hungry, Cousin Adelaide ! "

"You go and tell Mummy yourself before
tea, then," counselled Cousin Adelaide.

"But she'll be awful disappointed in me."

"She will be more disappointed if she hears
from Mrs. Yelverton first."

"S'pose so." Billy nodded gloomily. "Wish
Tommy's mother used her motor; then we
couldn't have run after her. But she says the
roads here are too rough, and she'd as soon
cross the Atlantic in a dory—that's what she
said. They've got six motors in New York."

Cousin Adelaide seemed unenthusiastic over the Yelvertons' cars.

"Run along, lamb, to your mother, and get it over," said she, with sudden firmness; and as Billy disappeared she rose.

From below the veranda railing a very spick-and-span Nan was emerging, but there was something un-Nanlike about her expression.

"Why Nan, dear," Cousin Adelaide exclaimed, thankfully, "I thought you were out!"

"Came home and got dressed," said Nan, sheepishly, "and been sitting under the veranda trying to come out and tell you I was sorry— and Mummy too. I was just hatefully rude and unreasonable about those dressmaking lessons, Cousin Adelaide, and I want to begin them straight off. Mr. Perry Earlwood said my skirt sagged down behind and I never want to hear that again from anybody! You see, I simply had a panic. I felt as if I must get that dress and dance in that play, and I was in a perfectly wicked rage when I couldn't, till Mr. Earlwood said that sketch was a perfectly horrid, unfashionable thing."

"Mr. Earlwood?" Cousin Adelaide stared.

"I'd lunch with him, out on the old road.

I don't wonder they call him a 'Magnet,' as Billy says; he's far more of one than even Johnston. He never even hinted that I'd been dreadful, but of course I knew I had. I'm going straight in now to explain to Mummy."

But Mrs. Addington did not need any explanation.

" My dear, I knew," she said. " And never mind it all now, for I'm sure you'll never do it again. You can see, Nan, what a perfectly miserable life you will have if you let yourself get so uncontrollably angry. I know what it is, for I used to go into most dreadful rages myself."

" You ? " Nan really gasped. " When ? "

" When first we came here, after your father died. You were all little, and I had no money for you, and I hated everything—everything."

" Not like me this morning ? "

" Exactly ! " Her mother nodded. " But Billy helped me, he was so tiny, and he needed me so. Then—oh, we got along ! "

" Billy was telling Cousin about the Gold Thread, and he said you never let yours go."

Nan's mother laughed ruefully.

" I'm afraid I often do, Nan. It hurts me when I can't give you an innocent frock or so. I get impatiently rebellious."

12

" Oh, me ! " said Nan. " And you're so brave. You make me horribly ashamed, Mummy. Gracious ! what's this ? "

" It's me, it's me," Billy burst in, wildly. " Tommy cried, so his mother isn't coming, and I'm fearful glad. And Cousin Adelaide says she thinks we've had enough of some kind of er-motions, and it would be nice if we all came downstairs and ate candy. It's Huyler's—and a boy brought it up just now ! "

CHAPTER XIII

COUSIN ADELAIDE TURNS FAIRY GODMOTHER

NAN ADDINGTON sat in somewhat gloomy state in the attic.

Mr. Perry Earlwood had been as good as his word, and his bundle of books on small fruit-farming had arrived ; but even the optimistic Nan had toiled through them blankly, and now sat gazing blankly at them. Fruit-farming, done as books advised, wanted money : " Money in lumps, real capital," Nan groaned, with conviction.

It was no wonder her mother and Wood had just been content to toil along in the strawberry garden by rule of thumb. It was the only possible thing to do ; and they, and Nan too, would just have to keep on doing it. There was no hope of a college career ever being earned from the study of Mr. Earlwood's books which airily suggested five thousand dollars as a starting point. " Mother never even *saw* five thousand dollars," Nan moaned, despairingly. " I don't suppose she's even made enough this summer to let me have French and dancing classes. I'll just have to go on in ordinary school with those girls who don't want to know *anything*! I don't see—— Goodness, Lil, what's the matter? "

" I've been looking for you everywhere," Lil panted, indignantly, up the garret stairs, with Billy at her heels. " I've something perfectly wild to tell you. Listen, Nan! Cousin Adelaide's arranged it with mother, and I'm going to New York with her next week! And you're going to have extra French and prepare-you-for-college classes with that Professor Hallam mother couldn't afford last year! "

" What? " said Nan. She cast Mr. Perry Earlwood's books into a disregarded heap.

" Yes, yes, yes! Isn't it too perfectly lovely and beautiful and sublime for both of us? I could dance for joy! "

" It's—unspeakable! " Nan took a long breath. " Dance, I should think so—so could I. Let's jig! " And solemnly the two did a breakdown, while Billy shrieked with excitement.

" Cousin says I'm to have classes too in New

York, and that there will be plenty of girls and lots of fun for me, even though I'm not out. Mother thinks it's a splendid chance for me, and she hopes it will do me good," Lil panted, as they dropped exhausted on a trunk.

"Of course it will." Nan fanned herself wildly with an old stove-cover. "But you'll have a perfectly elegant time, too. Only— oh, Lil, don't hate it here when you have to come back ! "

" Lil's going to make-er-lot-er-money," Billy chanted, suddenly."

"What ? " said Nan. " Silly Billy, that's not what she's going for."

" It's in New York they do make it." Billy bristled. " Tony Yelverton said his father got rich there all in one day. I don't see why Lil can't.

" My gracious ! " Nan exploded. " Lil, where's mother ? " But she was gone before Lil could answer, with every bit of exultation wiped off her face. The extra classes, the French, she could not do either of them, could never be out all day with Lil in New York and Rose gone away, and her mother left alone to do all the housework and the washing, leaving out herding Billy.

" Mother, I can't." Nan burst in on her

mother in the living-room. "I don't even want those classes. I mean you—you couldn't do it all alone, without Rose!"

If it was incoherent, Mrs. Addington understood. "Oh, my Nan," she said, chokily, "you haven't heard everything. Rose is going to stay with us all winter—Cousin Adelaide has done that, too. So you can have all your classes, and know I'm having just a peaceful rest at home."

Nan flopped into a chair. "Oh, mother, that's the best yet," she gasped. "You don't know—I came down those stairs just now like a—a burst balloon! Do you think we've all made a mistake and got to heaven? Where's Cousin Adelaide? I've simply got to thank her."

But there was more than thanking Cousin Adelaide to be done before Lil started for New York. A plain blue serge travelling suit arrived from a shop whose name made Lil gasp with realized dreams ; a hat, shoes, and coat, a new trunk with Lil's initials on it, and—crowning wonder!—a little fitted travelling bag. It was the plainest of the plain, but it filled Lil's cup of joy to the brim.

When her trunk was packed, and her new pale blue dressing-gown laid in the last thing, so as to be at hand when she and Cousin Adelaide arrived in New York, Lil sank on her bed, and looked up at Nan.

"You're not sad, are you, Nanny, that Cousin isn't taking you to New York too?"

"Gracious, no! What put that into your head?" Both girls had their backs to the door and the precious packed trunk, and if a small white object moved hastily between the two they did not notice it. Nan shut down the trunk-lid with a backward swing of her arm, and perched on the bed beside Lil. "I don't even want to go to New York," she remarked, practically. "I'd like to go to some of the theatres, but I'd simply hate meeting floods of girls all dressed up, and all strange. I'd truly sooner stay here. Hullo, Billy, Lil's all packed! You're too late to help."

Billy sat down on the new trunk and was ordered off. "Cousin says girls can't go out alone in New York—I heard her telling Mummy so," he observed. "They have to have a shangaroo! What's a shangaroo, Lil?"

Lil and Nan stared at each other blankly.

"Don't either of you know what it is?" Billy demanded. "Cousin said Lil would have one."

"Chaperon, he means," Nan shouted. "Oh, Billy, it's only a name for Cousin!"

"Thought it was some kind of a dog," Billy returned, with injury, and grasped the small black Doll who had wriggled in after him. "Lil will miss you, Dollar-pup," he informed the little dog.

"Well, I won't miss the Boarder," returned Lil, with some heat. "He jumped right on my chest in the middle of the night last week, and I nearly had a fit."

"Wonder where he is," said Billy, idly. "'Spect I'll go and see.   He ate all Mr. Bowser yesterday, and Cousin's going to send me a new one."

But at lunch it was a desperate Billy who burst in upon his family.

"Boarder's *lost*," he gasped.   "I can't find him—and I've been *everywhere*! And I believe he's poisoned or he's run over, because he doesn't never not come when I call!"

"Oh, Billy, no; he couldn't be," Mrs. Addington began.   But Billy was certain, and by degrees his dark fears infected the family. Even cousin Adelaide joined in the search; and Rose darkly hinted that the Boarder wasn't a lucky name, and she had always feared some disappearance which would never be cleared up. Search as they might, no bounding, fluffy-tailed little white dog was to

be found anywhere, and even Nan gave up the
hunt and followed Lil to her room to gloat
once more over her new belongings.

"Just like a trousseau, isn't it?" Lil purred
over her new dressing-bag.

"Just," Nan nodded. "Lil, I wonder if
you'll see Nettie Yelverton in New York?"

"Nettie won't be in my set," Lil returned,
haughtily. "Cousin knows all the nice New
York people, and the Yelvertons are just
nobodies. Of course I won't exactly tell Nettie
so——"

"Boarder," sobbed Billy, outside the door,
on his way to a fifty-ninth search of the attic,
"oh, Boarder!"

"I think I'll have to go and help him," Nan
cried, uneasily.

"Nonsense, Billy's just gone crazy! Boarder's
down at the shore, or out somewhere with
Wood. He'll turn up. Don't you think I
could just sail over Nettie a little in New
York? She was always so horrid about our
being poor, and all the rest."

"She was," Nan agreed, thoughtfully, and
had a sudden illumination. "Lil, I don't
believe I'd say one word to Nettie, if I were
you. It doesn't sound nice, somehow. I don't
believe mother would ever do it."

" Do you mean I can't even tell her Cousin says she won't be in my set ? "

" Not if you want to be like mother."

" Oh, bother ! " grudgingly. " Well, I won't, then. Only I'd just love to take her down. She boasts so much. But I suppose I'd be boasting worse if I were horrid to her. Oh, Nan, I feel dreadfully about leaving you, now it's so close ! Will you miss me horribly ? "

" Yes." Nan's lip quivered. " But I won't think of it. Oh, Lil, there are new blue bedroom slippers—you never put them into your trunk ! Goodness ! I wish Billy could find the Boarder. Can't you think of anywhere I could look ? "

Lil shook her head, lifted the cover of her grand new trunk, and stood paralysed. Inside it, comfortably snuggled down on the precious new silk dressing-gown and sound asleep, lay the missing Boarder.

" Billy," Nan screamed, " he's found ! Boarder's found ! Oh, don't, Lil," for Lil's hand was lifted to strike. " Can't you see he's quite stupid. He hasn't had enough air."

She seized the Boarder, shoved him into the arms of Billy, who wept on the attic landing, and shooed them both off down to Rose.

" My new things," Lil wailed. " They're ruined ! "

Nan took a flashlight survey of the outraged trunk.

" Nothing's hurt one bit," she returned, practically. " Don't be silly, Lil ; there's not a scrap of harm done. Thank goodness, you hadn't strapped the trunk for the morning, and left the Boarder to smother ! "

" It would have served him right "—wildly. " My new dressing-gown's all crumpled and creased, and there are two white hairs on it —and I know Boarder's feet were all dirty, even if I can't see their marks. I just adored those things, and I hate dogs. Billy "—Lil opened her door and shrieked furiously down the stairs —" Billy, don't you ever let the Boarder come near me or my room till I've gone ! "

" He wanted to go with you." Billy's indignant shriek rose piercingly in answer. " He only just packed himself up. He was clever —and I don't see why you're so fearful cross ! "

" Well, I do ! My best things were almost done for. I'll never let that dog even come near me again. I——"

Nan seized her forcibly and sat her down on her bed.

" There," she observed, firmly. " I said so ;

you're getting New Yorky and fussy already. Last week you would have just laughed because Boarder packed himself up, and you haven't even thought of laughing. I know you've got to get grown-up, but I don't see why you have to get fussy and *old*! Supposing your things had been spoilt, there's plenty of petrol in the world—and anything would have been better than having Billy broken-hearted about a lost dog. For goodness' sake, lock your trunk and sit on it."

"I didn't think of Billy," Lil began slowly; but Nan had whirled out of the room and downstairs.

"Wasn't it *funny*, Billy?" she cried, beaming on him where he sat on the veranda, watching the perfectly recovered Boarder taking a resuscitating roll on a flower bed. "Fancy Boarder being there all the time!"

But Billy clutched her.

"Oh, Nanny, I was frightened—terrible frightened! I had a dreadful inside think about Boarder. I love you, Nanny, more'n tongue can tell!"

CHAPTER XIV

NAN'S WINTER SUIT

NAN cast herself down on the top step of the veranda and gazed blankly at her mother and Billy.

"I really feel as if I couldn't stand any more partings," she announced, gloomily. "Billy, I hope if you or Doll and the Boarder intend to travel, you'll pack up and go away in the night so that I won't have to be harrowed by seeing you off. I've been doing nothing but say good-bye all day."

It was true. Dick and Frank Allen had gone off with Johnston Earlwood by the first train that morning, and Cousin Adelaide and Lil followed them in the afternoon. Nan had hoped Cousin Adelaide's last glimpse of the house would be in the golden glow of September sunshine, with the first torches of the maple leaves just lit and flaming; but a sea-mist had turned it all dull and dingy, till it seemed to Nan no memory to take away. Even Billy had said coming home from the station was just like coming from a funeral, and Nan set her lips not to agree. Lil had always been her best companion and playmate, and the sister who was left behind knew somehow that all that would never be just the same again. Lil would never be content at home after a winter in New York.

"You musn't even think it, Nan," Mrs. Addington said, less gaily than usual, for her head ached desperately, and the weeping Rose had seen fit to console herself for being left alone in a house that felt horribly empty by turning out the living-room and driving her mistress to the damp veranda. "Cousin Adelaide can give Lil so many advantages, and I couldn't refuse them."

"I know," Nan began, and broke off to point silently at Billy, sitting dissolved in tears on the steps. "It's his Gold Thread book," she whispered. "He gave it to Cousin for a parting present; I expect he wishes he hadn't, poor baby!"

"Oh, how could I be so stupid!" Mrs. Addington forgot her headache. "Fly, Nan, to my room for a parcel. Cousin left it to be given to Billy as soon as she was gone."

"For you, Billy," Nan cried, casting a flat, square parcel into his arms. "Cousin left it for you—hurry up and open it!"

But Billy was dumb. Inside the knotted string and the double wrappers lay the most wonderful thing in the world—a new Gold Thread book. There were pictures and pictures in it, shining in blue and scarlet and gold, even the cover was scarlet and gold, and Billy's old one had only been brown, even in the days when it was new and his mother was a little girl.

"Oh, mummy," was all he could gasp, "I didn't know there was any Gold Thread book like this! And Cousin has only got my old one!"

"That is what Cousin wanted," Nan assured him, laughing. "Now come on, and we'll forget good-byes. I have to go and help Wood cover the asparagus bed with sea-weed, and you can go and help him bring it from the shore with your wheelbarrow. Want to?"

But Billy had raced for his wheel barrow already, and had almost forgotten his tears in the joy of going off like a real man and conversing affably with Wood.

"I b'lieve it's frightful cheerful to go out and do a day's work," he announced that evening, as he and Nan came into the house ; and Nan looked round her and agreed with him.

Rose had finished her cleaning, there was a comfortable wood fire glowing in the living-room grate, the old red damask curtains were drawn cosily across the windows, and the lamp burned brightly on a table all laid for supper. Best of all, their mother was placidly reading by the fire, and it did Nan good to see her just sitting there while Rose attended to all the things Mrs. Addington had been used to do herself. There were no half-measures about Rose. Once she took hold her grip was steady, and nothing could stop her from accomplishing all she meant to do.

" Blackberry day to-morrow," Nan said, gaily. " Mother, you'll come, won't you ? I wonder how much I'm going to make out of my own money-patch this year."

" Oh, I'll come," Mrs. Addington returned. Nan's own money-patch was a thicket of wild blackberries she had discovered and cared for herself. Two years ago she had got Wood to cut away the undergrowth that encroached on it, and dig and manure the soil, till now Nan's blackberry crop was far finer than any her mother had ever seen, and the big luscious berries were safe to coin Nan's winter frock for her. " I think we'll take Rose too, and make a day of it," Mrs. Addington suggested. "Billy, are you going to bring Tommy Yelverton, like last year ? "

" He won't come," Billy returned, gloomily. " Tommy and me's had a fight. He said the Boarder wasn't thoroughbred, and he is, too ; he's a thoroughbred cur, the Magnet said so. And he was awful angry because I wouldn't swop my red aigine for his steamer that goes in water, and he went round the house where I couldn't see him, and he made the Boarder scream like being murdered with putting burrs in his nice white tail, and Nan came out and said he was a nasty little boy, and to go straight home. And then he was awful angry with Nan. He said he didn't want to help pick her sour old blackberries, and he was going to pay her out for calling him names."

" What a tempest in a tea pot," Nan commented, scornfully. " I never called him any names; nasty little boy was only just true ! You'd better go over, Billy, and tell him to come to-morrow, all the same."

" He won't, Nanny. He said he'd rather play with the village boys than me, and he isn't speaking to me."

" Well, let him," said Nan. " He'll get over

it. We'll start right after breakfast without him, Billy Boy, and when we wake up it's going to be a fine day."

It was ; and by ten o'clock Billy and the Boarder and the small black Doll were heading the procession to the blackberry patch, Billy almost hidden by his burden of empty baskets. Rose was laden with mysterious bundles of lunch whose contents she refused to tell anyone. Nan carried two pails and a kettle, and only Mrs. Addington, who was the guest of honour, carried nothing—unless you counted a bottle of dioxygen for the wasp stings Billy was bound to get.

The day was lovely, all soft sunshine and exhilarating wind, with just a hint of crispness. The sumacs waved great crimson plumes over the thickets of yellowing bracken as the expedition climbed the hill to Nan's blackberry patch, and Billy burst out suddenly :

"Looks just as if we were really going to the King's Palace in my Gold Thread book, with all the leaves turned red and yellow like flags along the road ! It's a lovely percession, and I'm the music. You listen!" He stumped ahead with his two small dogs, and his small voice floated back piping his "brave hymn" :

" ' Mocked, imprisoned, stoned, tormented,
     Sawn asunder, slain with sword.
They have conquered death and Satan,
     By the might of Christ their Lord.' "

Rose ran on and joined in. Nan dropped back
by her mother's side.

" Funny little soul Billy is," she smiled,
" but he's dreadfully sweet, mummy ! I wonder
how much we'll get for my berries this year ;
there ought to be a great many more than we
ever had, and I do need a new winter suit.
I'd hate to go all to my grand classes in Lil's
old one. The skirt's all wrong. And you'll
have to have a new hat, mother ; I saw one
at Miss Hunt's that would just suit you. We've
got to think of the Thanksgiving turkey, too,
and get that ; though it won't be a really
gay Thanksgiving without Lil," rather dolefully.

" Don't forget the Allen boys will be back
for it."

" Oh, I did ! And I promised them they
could come over and make candy. What
colour suit should I get, mummy ? "

" You'd look nice in a good dark blue."

" I'm tired of dark blue—it's so useful "—
rebelliously. " I'd like something light and

extravagant, one of those lovely new pale fawns that won't wear ! "

" Why, Nan ? "

Nan laughed in her mother's protesting face.

" I know I can't have it, but I'd just love to. Are you tired, mummy ? Because we're nearly there."

Golden rod pranked the side of the road with lavish riches, and Nan stuck a bit of it in her sweater as she spoke. Her mother slipped an arm through the girl's as they crossed a wide pasture, and came out in a mossy glade, full of sunshine between the topaz birch-trees, and ending in a rocky bank up which lay the path to the blackberry patch.

The blackberry owners put down their burdens. Rose cleared the fallen leaves from the rocks where she always made her fire, and Billy was assuring his mother that they had passed the lion in the way all right, just as the beloved Eric had passed him in the Gold Thread, when Tommy Yelverton burst wildly out of the bushes and tore past him, followed by a rabble of village boys, out of school for Saturday morning. Hot, dirty, and dishevelled the whole arty fled by the Addingtons and down the learing towards home, as if Billy's lion had chased them.

"Tommy!" Billy shrieked after him. "Stop! Come along and have lunch. We're going to pick blackberries."

Tommy did stop.

"You go and *look* at your old blackberries, Billy Addington," he shouted. "You'll be sorry, you and your old sister! I said I'd pay her out for calling me names."

"What on earth does he mean?" Nan stood rigid. "Tommy, come here this instant."

But Tommy and his friends had vanished into space. Nan turned to her mother.

"Come and look, mother. I can't wait to have lunch. Rose can get it," and she was gone, up the path Tommy Yelverton had come down.

Mrs. Addington and Billy scrambled after her, and in front of the blackberry patch Nan's mother stood aghast. The berries Nan had tended so faithfully were gone; most of the bushes were knocked flat, and on the ground, tramped down wantonly, lay mashes of black pulp, that had once been the shining, dark berries that were to buy a winter suit. Mrs. Addington stood paralysed, staring at the ruins. It was Billy who broke the silence.

"Tommy!" he roared, scarlet with fury, his blue eyes streaming with tears of rage.

"Tommy's did it—he said he'd pay Nan out ! "

Nan never opened her lips. Dead white, choking, she stared wordlessly at the awful ruin.

Their mother looked from one to the other and waited as speechlessly as Nan. If they were angry so was she, but there was no good in saying that. She put her arms round Billy as he crept to her for comfort ; but Nan, with one gasping sob, ran away : through her once-cherished blackberry patch, up into the wood above them—anywhere, to be out of sight, before she blazed out over one spiteful little boy. Her mother's new hat was gone, her suit, everything, unless—" I could go and tell Mr. Yelverton what Tommy's done, and let him pay for it." Nan clenched her teeth where she lay buried in the golden bracken. It would serve Tommy right, and she would have her money. But—" I can't, I can't ! " she burst out, amid frantic sobs she could not keep down.

Whatever she was fighting she fought out alone. She was quiet when she came back to the others, if her eyes were red, but the zest of the day was gone. Rose wailed over the almost untouched luncheon, and slipped away ith Billy to pick the one small clump of un-injured berries that remained in the patch.

"That's just nothing," Nan said, as the two returned with their harvest of two small baskets, but she could not go on. Even the useful dark-blue suit, quite beyond her reach, seemed a dream of joy now that it was impossible to get it.

"I guess we can't have turkey for Thanksgiving," Billy remarked, soberly, which did not mend matters.

"What are you going to do about it, Nannie?" Mrs. Addington asked.

"Nothing," said Nan, slowly. "I thought at first—oh, mother, I thought I could never forgive Tommy Yelverton, if he *is* only a child. You can't guess how I felt. Fifty evil spirits seemed to have got into me, and I just couldn't fight my awful temper. Till—I remembered Billy's ' brave hymn '—that was all."

Nan's mother looked at her quiet face, and thought it was a very great deal.

CHAPTER XV

BILLY'S TURKEY

" Rose ! " Billy stood in Rose's tidy kitchen one wet afternoon shortly before Thanksgiving. " Rose ! "

But for once Rose took no notice of him where she sat by the fire knitting. She had more to think of than she cared about, and was slowly screwing herself up to write a letter to Cousin Adelaide.

" Only I don't know how to begin," she pondered, doubtfully. " ' Dear Honourable Mrs. Sinclair ' is the right way, I guess. ' Mrs. Addington is having those attacks of pain, and the children don't know, and she won't have the doctor. I——' What, Billy?" impatiently.

" Rose, isn't there truly going to be any turkey for Thanksgiving ? "

" Good land, how do I know ? There's no sense in a little boy's fussing over it anyhow, Why don't you go and play with Tommy Yelverton ? "

" It's been pouring raining all the afternoon, and mother won't let me out. Tommy and I aren't speaking, anyhow, since he spoiled Nan's blackberries. And I haven't anything to do. Nan's dressmaking, and she's sewn the sleeves in wrong ; she's awful cross "—gloomily. " I think dressmaking isn't nice. What do you think ? "

" It's nice when you get on all right "—practically. " I'd admire to be making a new dress this minute."

" Don't feel as if I'd like it "—dolefully. " Makes people all say, ' Go away and don't bother.' You might tell me a story, Rose. I haven't got anything to *do*."

" Why don't you forgive Tommy ? You'll have to some time ! "

" Well, he's just got to see how horrid he was "—heatedly. " Mother said I mustn't tell him he really stole Nan's new dress and the Thanksgiving turkey by spoiling our blackberries, but I won't play with him till he says he's sorry."

" I shouldn't wonder if he was," Rose said, slowly. " He hangs round enough. He's for ever outside the gate. I'd go out and see him, Billy."

" Suppose I might as well forgive him." Billy

sighed. " But it's too rainy to go and look for him now. Do tell me a story, Rose."

" Oh my ! Well, once upon a time," droned Rose.

" There was a boy named Eric," Billy interrupted, ungratefully.

" No, no, it's not that story. It's one about a fairy prince and a princess."

" I know all about them, too ! " Billy exclaimed. " Didn't they live happy ever after ? "

" Yes "—unwillingly—" I guess so."

" Did they have a good cook ? "

" My land, what put that into your head ? "

" Mr. Yelverton "—in that gentleman's own pompous voice—" says most homes are ruined by bad food."

" Well, I never," Rose gasped. " Oh, yes, the prince and princess had a good cook, all right. Have a doughnut, Billy ? "

Billy shook his head. " I'd like a story about wolves—something nice and exciting."

" You go to that door and meet the postman instead. He's there, for I heard him," Rose suggested, desperately.

The bait took and Billy vanished, to rush in to his mother and Nan, waving a letter.

Nan put down the sleeves she had just sewed in for the fourth time.

" It's from Lil, mother," she said, happily. " Oh, do read it."

" Three sheets," Billy gasped as his mother opened Lil's letter. " I don't believe I'll ever write one as long as that. Is it all for you ? "

" It's for all of us. ' Dearest mother and the children,' " Mrs. Addington began, and Nan jumped.

" Children, I like that," she cried. " Never mind, mummy, go on. It doesn't matter if Lil calls us Hottentots. What does she say ? "

" ' I know you'll want to hear all our adventures, and there's so much to tell you I hardly know how to begin. Only, first, Cousin remembered Nan had no winter suit for those classes, and she's sending her one. It's lovely, and the latest fashion, but not too stylish for every day. There are gloves and stockings to go with it, and tell Nan she'll look splendid.' "

Nan started up and pirouetted all round the room.

" Oh, mother, isn't it too lovely of Cousin, and I am thankful I didn't tell about Tommy. Oh, when do you think my parcel will come ? "

" Shall I go down to the express office and see if it's there ? " Billy was almost as excited as Nan.

" No, it's too wet. And just knowing it's coming is simply perfect. I've felt so horrid and little in Lil's old suit. The girls all have such nice clothes this year I hardly dared lift my eyes up, but now I'll enjoy looking at them. There's a frightfully *confident* feeling about new clothes, and I'll write to Cousin and tell her so. Go on with the letter, mummy."

" ' Mother, the Perry Earlwoods' house is lovely. I told you all about our meeting them at the junction when I wrote before, and about going to New York with them in their private car, and I thought that was luxurious, but it is nothing to their old house in Madison Avenue. Nothing in it looks new, like the Yelvertons', and it's funny that the whole effect is so much grander. We go there a lot, but in a way I almost like Cousin's apartment better. She says it's a bit high up, but she likes that, as we have such big rooms and lots of air. I have the *sweetest* bedroom ! It's just like the kind in a story book that the only daughter has when she comes back from college, all pink roses on white everywhere, and of course my own bathroom— think of that, Nan, when Billy keeps you waiting

in the hall. Cousin has her own maid, besides
the other servants ; she is French, named Marie,
and as grand as a queen. It's a heavenly bless-
ing Cousin didn't bring her to stay with us ; we
would have expired with mortification. But
she does my hair here, and I can tell you it looks
lovely. She thinks I'm pretty—of course you
will all know I am only telling you what she
says, to show you the sort of *impression* I am
making : I don't think anything of my looks
since I've seen the perfectly beautiful girls
Cousin knows. They're so *chic*—Marie's word
—and I am not. But Cousin has given me six
new dresses—think of that ! I'll have to
describe them to you later, for we are going to
a matinée with the Earlwoods now, and I have
to get dressed in my loveliest dress of all. It's
dark-blue *velvet.* I'm so excited about everything that I can hardly write. The Earlwoods
have no daughter, only one other boy besides
Johnston. They did laugh so when Cousin told
them how Billy called him the Magnet. I am
going to begin some classes next week, but truly
so far I can't fix my mind on education ; it is
all too like fairyland. I feel a country mouse
in it, though ; I can't talk of one thing the other
girls talk of, and they are all so beautifully
dressed that I feel as if I ought to say arrayed,

but not a bit like Nettie dresses. I believe
they'd · die rather than go out in a diamond
side-comb. Cousin has a lovely auto-motor,
she calls it—with two servants, a chauffeur and
a man to open the door. She nearly always
takes me out in it. She looks fearfully elegant
always, but she keeps on telling me how she
loved staying with us; and truly, mother, I can't
understand how she *could* when I see how she
lives here.

"'Tell Billy New York is fine, and he'd love
to see the children riding ponies in the Park.
Cousin says hardly anyone has come back yet,
but of course she belongs to the old-fashioned
set, who only think about family. She doesn't
go in for new people at all. But it is just
splendid staying with her; and thank you ever
so much, mummy dearest, for letting me come.
Johnston Earlwood wants to be remembered to
you all, and he says he loved being at our house,
too. Isn't it funny? Every one seems to like
what they haven't got. And he says Billy is
a crackajack and Nan too. Ever your loving
daughter-sister, LIL.'"

"Is that all?" demanded Billy, and Nan
laughed.

"Isn't it enough? I feel as if I'd been at a
play."

" And I feel as if Billy had better be learning his lessons," his mother put in, warningly, " or he'll be kept in to-morrow."

But Billy's thoughts were not on lessons; Thanksgiving and no turkey weighed too heavily on his small mind. Such a thing had never happened in all his short life. Cousin's letter held no hope of turkey; Rose gave him cold comfort by saying turkey was out of fashion; only Nan, leaving him to dawdle home alone from school the day before Thanksgiving, hurried home and up to her mother's room to speak about him.

" Mother, to-morrow will be Thanksgiving," she said, bluntly. " What are we going to do about a turkey? "

" I don't know." Mrs. Addington turned round rather slowly. " I don't think we can have one. Do you mind much, Nan? "

" No "—carelessly. " But Billy does— dreadfully."

" I'm afraid you'll mind too when I tell you you must have the two Allen boys to dinner even without turkey! Mr. Allen came in this morning to say he and his wife were suddenly called away—and would I have the boys to Thanksgiving dinner? "

" *Mother!* What did you say? "

"What could I say? You wouldn't have liked me to refuse!"

"No." Nan sounded doubtful. "But how shall we do it?"

"Oh, Rose will manage—somehow. Surely, Nan, you wouldn't leave those poor boys with nowhere to go, simply because we haven't any turkey!"

"No," said Nan, frankly. "But what I can't see, mother, is why we can't have one. We always did—long before I thought of having any blackberry money."

"I know." Mrs. Addington's face changed. "But things have—oh, Nan, I'm worried! Fielding the grocer owes us such a lot of money. You see, so many of his summer people run up bills with him, and then take a long time to pay. He has had nearly all our summer vegetables, and he has only paid me about a quarter of what he owes for them. I don't know quite what to do—except to keep out of debt myself."

"But you'll get it? You don't mean you're afraid he won't pay you at all?" Nan gasped.

"I don't know—I'm uneasy! I only told you, Nanny, because you are always such a help to me."

"A help? Me?" Nan stared. "When I all

but said I didn't want to have the Allen boys
as we had no turkey ! "

" You're a help, all the same." Mrs.
Addington laughed a little. " I feel so proud
of my daughters, Nan. Cousin Adelaide says
Lil is doing so well, and you are a real prop to
me."

" I miss Lil dreadfully, mummy." Nan's
voice shook.

" But you don't grudge her all the pleasure
she's having ? "

" Grudge it—to Lil ? Oh, *no* ! I love her
to have it. Do let's go downstairs, mummy,
it's cold up here. Just hear the wind, and the
ground must be frozen—there's a cart simply
rattling over the road past the gate. Come
along down."

Rose came out of the kitchen as they
descended.

" Billy's out late," she said, crossly, shoving
wood into the big hall stove. " I can't see
what's become of him."

" Isn't he in ? " his mother exclaimed, sharply.
" Why, Rose, it's nearly dark ! Do you suppose
he's been kept in ? "

" He never is," said Nan. " He's far
ahead of his class always. I'd better go and
see, mother."

14

But as she jumped for her coat the outside door flew open. A gust of wind, Billy, and the two dogs, who always waited for him at the gate, burst in together.

"I've got a turkey," Billy shrieked. His cheeks scarlet, and his little button of a nose crimson with cold, he cast down a huge bundle at Rose's feet. "Just *look* at it—it's fine!"

"But how? You haven't been doing something dreadful to make a lot-er-money?" Nan burst out at him.

"No! Oh, mummy, it's just like a fairy story." Billy danced up and down with glee. "I was coming home from school and I dropped one of my books, and a funny old gentleman had picked it up and was looking at it when I ran back for it. At least I think he was old—he said he was. I said 'Yes, sir,' when he asked me if my name was Billy Addington, and he said good something, how time flies, and he used to know another one. And to tell my mother I'd met Frank Parker, and he'd be over to-morrow to see her, because he was spending Thanksgiving with his nephew here, and here was ten cents for taking the message."

"Frank Parker!" exclaimed his mother. "Come all the way from California, at his age! Oh, I shall be glad to see him; he was one of the best old friends your father ever had. Only, Billy, I don't see how his ten cents got you a turkey "—suddenly.

" It did." Billy bounced up and down before her like an India-rubber ball. " His ten cents was a five *dollar* gold piece. And I bought a turkey ! "

" But, my land "—Rose seized the brown-papered turkey and held it up—" I don't see how you ever came home with it. It's sixteen pounds, if it's one."

Billy beamed at her. " Oh, the express man drove me to the gate," he returned, simply— " the one you went out with last Sunday.

CHAPTER XVI

NAN BLOSSOMS OUT

THERE was no doubt of the success of the Thanksgiving party. Frank and Dick Allen interpreted their invitation literally, and arrived early to spend the day, and to build Billy an Indian camp down by the shore for a winter plaything. Nan disappeared mysteriously as soon as it was finished, and Dick Allen, returning hot and hungry with his brother and Billy, stood stock still as he went up the veranda steps.

Nan was waiting for them at the door; only it was a new Nan, and the boy could only stare at her. Her untidy, curling hair was plaited in two shining ropes and brought tight round her small head, and her cheeks were as softly pink as the pink *crêpe* frock she wore.

"Nan!" said Dick Allen. "But—why, you're simply scrumptious!"

"I've had the pink stuff for ages," Nan

explained, hastily. "And Cousin Adelaide gave me dressmaking lessons."

"D'ye mean you made it, all yourself?" Dick demanded. "Well, I always said you were the cleverest girl I knew!"

"I'm not," returned Nan, with some heat. "Only, tell me, Dick! Don't I look beautifully grown-up?"

"You look very pretty," Frank Allen announced, bluntly, from the step behind his brother. "I'm quite afraid of such an elegant young lady. Billy, what on earth do you suppose has become of Tomboy Nan?"

"I'll take it all off if you tease," said the heroine of the occasion, with a sudden ominous gasp.

Dick Allen plumped down on his knees in front of her.

"Don't, Nan! And do forgive us, we were only joking. But you do look stunning with your hair like that.

"Get up, you ridiculous creature!" But Nan turned her head away with a sudden knowledge of something she had seen in Dick's eyes.

"Well, I never thought old Nan would be such a beauty," Frank Allen announced with the candour of the boy chum. "I thought Lil was the pretty one. But Nan's a fizzer. Don't you learn to cut out any more, Nan. You can cut out anyone, now ! "

" What a back-number joke ! " Nan jeered.

" No joke at all. It's a fact. Why, you're the ' Oh, you ought to have seen her ' girl now ! "

" Let me look," Billy burst out, and turned away. " I don't see any difference," he announced, with disappointment. " She's only just Nan. You wait till you see my turkey ; it's as grand as a queen ! "

Dick Allen chuckled, and swept him off to be washed. But even Billy was silent as they sat down to dinner. Rose had surpassed herself ; even the great golden-brown turkey almost paled before the mounds of cranberry jelly, and the sweet potatoes, fried as only Rose could fry them.

" Such a lovely dinner never was," Billy sighed over his last plate of ice-cream. " I'm glad it's cold and going to snow out of doors. I feel as if I only wanted to sit by the fire and tell stories."

" Well, do," said Mrs. Addington, " and I'll begin with a true one. What will you say, Billy and Nan, when I tell you I am going to New York in the morning ? "

"Mother," Nan shrieked. "But me—and Billy?"

"That is what's worrying me. I can't take you. You and Billy will just have to take care of the house and each other."

"I wish Frank and I were going to be here to look after them, Mrs. Addington." Dick Allen looked very tall and grown-up where he stood by the fire. "But we have to go too."

Nan stared from one to the other. She had no idea how she was to get on without her mother, nor what on earth could be taking her to New York. "But why——" she began, and bit her lip.

"I'll tell you all about it presently, Nannie; it's nothing to worry about," Mrs. Addington said, hastily. "Listen, wasn't that someone at the door?"

"My turkey man!" Billy scrambled up wildly. But his mother shook her head.

"He was here this morning, dear old man," she said. "It's——"

"Tommy and Nettie Yelverton," Billy gasped, blankly. He had not spoken to Tommy since the dreadful spoiling of the blackberries, but he said, "Hullo, Tommy! Want to come and popcorn?"

Tommy said he didn't care if he did, while

Nettie explained volubly that none of their expected guests had arrived; even Tony had never turned up. And it was so dull and dreary, she and Tommy had come over to say good-bye—they were off to New York in the morning.

"Well, take off your things and stay," Nan suggested, hospitably. "Mother, let's dance, now Nettie's here."

Mrs. Addington went to the piano, as the boys rolled up the rugs and pushed back the furniture. Nan and Dick danced exquisitely, and even Billy and Tommy forgot their popcorn and joined in the fray, till Nettie and Frank danced over them, and Dick created wild amusement by insisting on dancing with Rose in the kitchen, though she told him to go along —she had done with such foolishness. But all the same she improvised an impromptu supper that even Nettie Yelverton admired, as well as Nan's pink dress, which she supposed was a present from Cousin Adelaide in New York, till the candid Nan undeceived her.

"Been a great day all round," Dick Allen observed, with a wink at Nan, "and time to get out now; Mrs. Addington looks tired."

Mrs. Addington looked more than tired when the visitors had taken themselves off, and Billy had gone to bed, but she pulled Nan's chair close to hers and laid a hand on the girl's.

"Now we'll talk, Nannie," she said, softly. "I didn't mean to startle you just now, but I was rather startled myself. You see, Cousin Adelaide wrote yesterday, and Lil wired this morning for me to go to her."

"What *for*? She's not ill or anything?"

"No," said her mother, shortly. "She's worried. Johnston Earlwood wants her to marry him, and she doesn't know what to say."

"What?" said Nan. "Do you mean she doesn't like him—not like *Johnston*?"

"I don't know, dear; how could I? But Lil and Cousin Adelaide seem to be all in a muddle, and want me to come and straighten things out. Cousin says Lil won't talk to her as she would to me, and sent me money for my ticket, and I feel that I have to go. Remember, this is all in strict confidence, Nannie."

"I'll keep it secret." Nan squeezed her mother's arm. "Only I do think—— Why, it's perfectly *silly* for Lil to send for you to make up her mind for her."

"It's not that"—hastily. "It's that wretched Tony Yelverton. I gather he's told Lil she is the only girl who can ever make anything of him, and that he'll do something

desperate—oh, you know how impossible he
could be. And Cousin says Lil believes him ! "
    " That's the silliest yet," Nan burst out,
indignantly. " Oh, dear, what an awful bother
girls are, growing up and getting married. I'm
never going to do it, having lovers hanging
round would be too tiresome ! "
    Mrs. Addington had to laugh. " You've more
commonsense than Lil," she said, easily. " She
never told you anything about it all, did
she ? "
    " Never mentioned it," rather huskily. " I
—mummy, it's good of you to tell me. I—
never can say much to you, you know."
    " I know ; I couldn't either, when I was a
girl. Do you know, Nannie, that when my
mother told me my father was dying I had
simply nothing to say. I just stood tongue-
tied. I've often thought of it since—often
longed to tell her how I felt then, but I never
could speak. I'm glad you and I aren't like
that."
    " She knew," Nan flung out, passionately,
" you'd know ! Now, mummy, tell me what
you want me to do."
    " We're talking as if I were going to discover
the South Pole "—Mrs. Addington kissed her
between tears and laughter—" instead of going

to New York for a week. I don't want you to do anything but look after Billy ; Rose will see to the house. I've told her I was going, but not why."

"It will do you good." Nan sat up and shook herself. " You need the change, and we won't have time to miss you dreadfully. Only, truly, I don't see how you're going to arrange for Lil."

"Lil must do her own arranging," Mrs. Addington said, unexpectedly. " I would not dare to interfere. She's too young to marry anyone, unless she cares a great deal for him."

"You married at eighteen—and Lil's nearly that ! "

" Yes "—quietly. " But you see I am so wise now that I know Lil is a little different from what I was at her age."

" I don't see why she has to fuss about getting married at all," Nan exploded, rebelliously. " She won't be ours any more, and she'll always be thinking about Johnston, even if she has to wait for him. I did think Johnston Earlwood had more sense than to be fussing round, falling in love ! And I don't see where that wretched Tony comes in ! "

" Cousin says "—but Mrs. Addington laughed,

it sounded so snobbish—" that it's because Lil goes to houses he could never get into. Don't worry about Tony, Nan."

" I'm not," said Nan, absently. " Mother, I'm nearly as tall as you, and my new skirt's pretty long for me. Do take it and the coat —the new one Cousin gave me—to wear in New York ! You know you haven't a thing fit to go out in, and Cousin's friends are so elegant, and—you must have known them all once ! "

" Till they forgot me "—rather quietly. " It is dear of you to offer me your things, but I couldn't take them. I'm not likely to go out much in New York."

But Nan was staring at her with sudden illumination. " Mother, I never thought," she burst out. " It must have been awful for you when father died, and you had to come out here and struggle on with us, all alone ! Wasn't there *anyone* who stood by you ? "

" Nobody much. But—oh, yes, it was hard, Nannie ! But I've won through now ; and I have you, and Billy, and Lil."

" And we're going to lose her " said Nan, ruefully.

" We can't expect her to stay with us for ever, but I agree with you that it's too soon for her to go yet. Why, *Nan*, what are you doing?"

"No grown-up for *me*," returned her younger daughter, concisely. Four large, and stolen, hairpins of her mother's flew down on the rug, and her small, tightly coiled head turned magically to a waist-deep mantle of red-brown curls. "I've decided to become a celebrated dancer, and *never* marry!"

But, oddly enough, as she turned away to fly upstairs and do her mother's packing before she went to bed, Mrs. Addington thought Nan had never looked so womanly.

CHAPTER XVII

BILLY

" WELL, that's over," said Nan, rather forlornly. She took Billy's hand as the morning train rolled out of the station with their mother on board, and the two trudged up the road towards home; Billy was snuffling as he led Doll and Boarder, whose lives had been too precious to risk unchained near a train, and Nan was shivering in Lil's last year's suit. But as she looked down at it Nan laughed. Her own new suit, warm and pretty, lay in the bottom of Mrs. Addington's trunk, without that lady's knowledge.

" And she'll have to wear it, and look nice," her daughter thought, gaily. " And, anyhow, she is only going to be away a week ! "

But, all the same, the house seemed remarkably flat and dreary when she and Billy returned from school and classes in the early dark of the afternoon, and it seemed drearier as the next days crawled by. Rose's ultimatum that

" you're to do just as you would if your ma was here " was wasted, to her secret dismay. Nan took up all her mother's duties—an example of unearthly piety which was promptly followed by Billy. He wiped his boots when he came in, learned his lessons without grumbling, and got up in the morning without being called ; just as Nan's devotion to the mending basket was almost saintly, and her sewing conducted without so much as a snip left on the living-room floor— a condition of things which was so unnatural that Rose would have found life incredibly dull if it had not been for two unfortunate blows : Mrs. Sinclair had never sent her month's wages, and Fielding the grocer, from whom Mrs. Addington had deputed Rose to get the money owing for her summer produce, had never sent one cent. Rose was nothing if not a faithful steward. She trudged over to the grocer's one bitter afternoon, after sending two notes and getting nothing, and got very little more. Fielding either would not, or could not pay. After an hour's acrimonious battle, Rose was obliged to retire with nothing more than five dollars' worth of groceries on Mrs. Addington's contra account.

She was really angry. Fielding had had a week's grace on the date when he had promised to pay Mrs. Addington in full; the butcher's bill was owing, the winter coal to be paid for, and no money in hand for the housekeeping odds and ends no grocery store could supply. Rose, returning home chilled and weary, poked up the kitchen fire viciously.

"Praise mercy the coal's here, paid for or not," she said, crossly, to Nan, in the kitchen door. "Tea ain't ready, if that's what you want. For the land's sake, sit down and wait with Billy."

"Billy's come home from school with the earache." Nan took no notice of the snap. "Come and look at him. I'm afraid he's going to have croup."

"Croup don't begin in ears," Rose returned, disdainfully. But she was at Billy's side almost as she spoke with warm oil and hot flannel, and hustled him off to bed. Towards ten o'clock she went up to look at him, hoping to find him asleep. But Billy was dolefully wakeful. His ear was feverishly and miserably worse, and when he finally did go to sleep it was in Rose's comforting arms.

"He can't be going to no school to-day," Rose informed Nan in the morning. "He has a cold all over, and I'll keep him with me."

Nan assented with a self-absorbed grunt.

Her work for the history class was not ready ; she had slept during the morning hours when she meant to study, and got up cross ; and a letter from Lil had made her crosser, though it was only to say she and her mother had been to a luncheon at the Earlwoods', and " Mother looked quite nice in your new suit."

" Quite nice ! "—Nan shivered herself aggrievedly into Lil's old one, which had never been warm even when it was new—" and me going out to *freeze* ! I think Mother might have written again, and told me where she'd been in my clothes. I—oh, there, I've broken my bootlace ! "

It was too late to look for another. Nan went down to breakfast with a knot digging into her ankle, scolded Rose for not calling her, snapped at Doll and the Boarder for getting in her way, and went off to her classes, furious with herself and with Rose for laughing at her. It was five when she returned, and for once Nan did not search out Billy, who was in the kitchen with Rose, but cast herself down by the fire with a book. She was fathoms deep in the " Tale of Two Cities " when a small voice at the door startled her.

" Nan," said Billy, hoarsely, " I can't find Doll and the Boarder. Rose won't let me go

15

out and call them, and I'm afraid they've gone somewhere."

" All right." Nan never looked up. " In a minute—when I've finished this chapter— I'll go and find them."

" But, Nan, they——"

" They're all right," said Nan, impatiently. " I'll go in a minute." But one page and another turned under her absorbed fingers, the chapter slid imperceptibly into another, till a slow, insidious drift of cold air brought the reader to aggrieved feet. " Who on earth——" began Nan, and was at the front door with one jump. It was wide open to the cold, dark, and sleeting rain. " Billy ! " Nan shouted. " My goodness, he's gone *out* ! " Hatless and coatless, she dived out after him into a bitter wind that chilled her to the bone.

But nowhere was there any sign of Billy.

" Doll, Boarder, Billy," Nan called, peremptorily, flying down the garden path to the stable, to Wood's tool-house, to the wood-shed. But as Billy could not open the wood-shed door, there was no sense in looking there ! She was turning away when a voice smote her through the dark.

" *Nan*, come here quick ! I hear them— they're inside ! "

Nan pounced, and seized a drenched small

boy struggling valiantly with the wood-shed bolt.

" Go back to the house—quick ! " she commanded. " You'll catch more cold. Run ! I'll get the dogs out."

But the stiff bolt stuck even under Nan's strong fingers. How long she wondered, had a little boy been struggling with it in the sleet and cold, while she was lost in a book by the fire ? It took even Nan five minutes to free the captives, who fled for the house and Billy, as if they had been away for years. Nan, racing after them, found Rose had captured Billy, soaked to the skin, and was putting him to bed.

But his teeth kept on chattering even when he was wrapt in a blanket and drinking hot lemonade. Nan gave a despairing glance at him.

" It's my fault, Rose," she wailed. I was reading, and I didn't go for the dogs when he asked me to. Why didn't you *make* me, Billy ? "

" I couldn't. I didn't believe you'd *ever* go," Billy gasped. ' I knew they'd be in the wood-shed—they go there to hunt mice, and Wood shuts the door on them—and they're afraid there in the night "

Rose glanced at him in her turn, and forebore

to scold ; and by bedtime she was too worried. Billy had pain in his side, and a temperature. Nan hung over him in a tempest of regret and remorse.

" I'll get the doctor in the morning if he's no better," she said, miserably, and Rose nodded.

But with the morning it was very evident he was worse, and Nan flew off before breakfast to fetch Dr. Marsh. But Dr. Marsh, for once, was no comfort. All he would say was that Billy had pleurisy, and that he would be back before night. Nan stared at Rose as the door shut behind him

" Mother will be back in two days " she said, hopefully.

" And I'll be glad to see her as I never was so glad for anything." Rose lifted her head to listen. " My land, Miss Nan, there's the postman now ; pray there's something from your ma about coming ! "

Nan flew into the hall, and stood there speechless. There was only one letter, and it was not from her mother, but Cousin Adelaide. And Cousin Adelaide said——

" Rose," Nan blurted, fiercely, " Mother isn't coming this week at all. Cousin Adelaide says she's in bed—that it's only a slight attack of grip, but she isn't fit for a cold journey."

Something like a cold hand touched Rose's honest heart.

" I guess you'll have to write to her to come as soon as she can," she said, slowly. " I don't mean Billy's so sick exactly—Dr. Marsh said I could do for him as well and better'n any trained nurse he wasn't used to—but the child's apt to fret for his ma, and he ain't such a strong little chap anyway. You write, Miss Nan, real careful, and say we'll do the best we can for a day or two, but it will be a mercy when Mrs. Addington gets home."

Nan, sitting with Billy all that day and the next, agreed with Rose. If ever a child needed his mother it was Billy. He tossed and turned and moaned as he lay in his feverish bed, pushed Rose's hot drinks and milk away from his cracked lips with his hot little hands.

" I want an orange," he whispered. " Oh, Nannie, couldn't you get me an orange ? My throat's so dry. I do want an orange ! "

" I know," Nan began helplessly, and glanced at Rose. " Fielding has none," she whispered. " I went this morning. He hadn't anything."

Billy began to cry, weakly and bitterly ; but there was something so quiet and resigned in the pitiful little face he hid in the bedclothes that Rose's heart rebelled.

" Fruit I'll have for him, if I tear Fielding's shop down," she said to Nan, fiercely. "Now, Billy, lamb, you wait. Rose will get you oranges—yes, and grapes ! "

She had her hat and coat on and was in the wagon almost before old Wood had the pony harnessed, and the hurricane created on her arrival at Fielding's shop will be remembered by that gentleman to the end of time. That he had no fruit availed him nothing. Rose got what she wanted by the simple method of dragging Fielding himself down the street to the rival establishment of the village, the window of which held fruit galore. Rose took hot-house grapes, grape fruit, oranges, lemons, made Fielding pay for them in hard dollars, and wrote him a receipt for the money

" And, next year " she asserted, for the benefit of all concerned, " no strawberries, asparagus, nor sweet corn do you buy from Mrs. Addington, while I'm within hail of her. No, sir ! She hasn't no need to give her stuff away, nor she isn't a charitable society for providing lazy grocers with green stuff, and don't you forget it. And you pay up quick, all you owe her, so's I don't have to haul you round by the collar like this again ! "

If it was a triumph, it was small comfort.

Day by day, almost hour by hour, in spite of Dr.
Marsh and of Rose, and Rose's good nursing,
Billy steadily grew worse.

"He's drifting away—out on that road to
the King's Palace, he's sure going," sobbed Rose.
"He talks about it, and he drives me near
crazy ; I feel as if I could screech. You don't
think he's getting ready for it, do you ? " she
besought Nan, who only swallowed hard and
could not answer. " Oh, I know he ain't quite
in his right head, but to hear him whispering
about that palace, and the road to the moon,
and his mother "—Rose paused and caught her
breath hard. " Well, there, I've cried and cried,
and I guess I've just got to stop ! I'll go and
make us some real strong coffee. I guess it'll
do us both good."

But even after the coffee neither Rose nor
Nan could hide from each other that they were
growing desperate. No letter at all had come
from Mrs. Addington in answer to the frantic
daily notes Nan had sent her, nothing from Lil,
nothing even from Cousin Adelaide, the punc-
tilious, but a casual telegram or two, saying
only, " Mother doing very well," or " Everything
all right ; don't be anxious."

" You might think we'd never even mentioned
to one of 'em that Billy was dying," Rose burst

out, " or else going to New York has turned
them all crazy ! Why, grip or no grip, I'd have
thought your ma would have been home on the
first train. Do you suppose she ain't even *read*
your letters ? "

Nan turned a white, curiously steady face to
Rose's weeping one.

" I don't believe she's ever had them, Rose,"
she said, slowly. " I—I think Mother must be
ill too—for all I know, nearly as ill as Billy—and
they're not letting her have her letters, or
anything that might worry her. Cousin
Adelaide's like that, you know—dreadfully
thorough ! I don't believe Mother knows."

" But, land's sake, your cousin and Lil
know ! What's the matter with one of them
coming ? You've wrote and told them often
enough. I don't see why one of 'em don't
even answer a letter. We've got to do something, right now to-day, that'll *make* 'em tell
your ma ! "

" I don't see what," said Nan, chokingly.
" I've telegraphed to Cousin Adelaide's flat
twice—once to her and once to Lil—and neither
of them have even answered me, unless those
" Mother better " wires of Cousin's are supposed
to be answers. I—I don't know what to do ! "

" I guess thēre ain't anything we can do. If

it's to be this way it's to *be* this way." Rose's voice was rougher than Nan had ever heard it. "I guess we'll pull through. He ain't dying yet, if he is bad. You go now and sponge his face for him careful, while I get a mite of rest."

But, for a person who had been night-nursing for a week, Rose took a queer way to rest. For ten long minutes she stood by the kitchen table, staring vacantly at its white oilcloth. It was over a fortnight since Mrs. Addington had left—but Rose suddenly nicked the days off on the kitchen calendar.

"My land, it's most three weeks!" she said, under her breath. "I've kind of lost count of the days while Billy's been so bad. It ain't natural, all this crazy not hearing; I've got to do something, and I just pray the Lord to show me what I *can* do!"

What indeed? Unknown to Nan, Rose had written twice, once to Mrs. Sinclair and once to Mrs. Addington, with no mincing of matters in her trenchant statements. If those had failed—"Well, I guess there ain't any way else to try," said Rose, dully, "except keep going. My land, that iron Nan left on the stove is white hot!"

Why she did not lift Nan's forgotten iron

with her asbestos iron holder was a mystery :
it hung directly in front of her. But instead
Rose knelt wearily at the cupboard where she
kept brown paper from the family parcels neatly
folded for future use. The thick piece on top
would do, the one with the printed white label
on it—the white label that had come—— But
suddenly, as she looked at it, something about
that white label leapt at Rose like a thing
alive.

" It's *it*," said she cryptically. " And even
if it ain't, I'll try it. Anyway, it's something
to do ! "

Whatever it was, she did it. But she never
took Nan's iron off the stove, nor scolded Nan
because it was ruined.

Both of them had other things to think of,
perhaps. The fluid on Billy's lungs, that increased instead of decreasing ; Dr. Marsh's frown
as he looked at him ; the three long days that
dragged by without a word from his mother ;
and worst of all, the night when Dr. Marsh came in
and told Nan he had telegraphed for a specialist
from New York, and expected him by the nine
o'clock train.

" But "—Nan clutched Dr. Marsh's arm as
he stood beside her in the forlorn living-room,
that for once had not been dusted for a week

—" Oh, Dr. Marsh, anything to save Billy ; I know ! But I—I haven't any money. I can't pay him ! "

" That's all right ; I'll manage that. Your mother can settle with me later on," but though Dr. Marsh's kind hand was on Nan's shoulder he was thinking of something else. " That boy's mother ought to know how very seriously ill he is, Nan ! Why on the earth doesn't she come home ? You can't have written plainly."

Nan stared at him blankly. Days and nights of worry and fear had taken all the colour from her face, and now something she dared not name took the courage from her heart. If Billy died it would be her fault, for letting him run out that day in the wind and sleet. And unless her mother came—for the first time Nan broke down.

" I can't help it about Mother," she sobbed. " I've written and written, and I believe she must be ill too, and they're not giving her her letters. She's never even answered mine about Billy, and Cousin Adelaide——" but with Cousin's name Nan burst out with all her misery : her long days of waiting for letters that never came, the desperate telegrams she was sure her mother had never received.

She'll get one from me, then," exclaimed Dr. Marsh, grimly, whisking a night letter form from his pocket and beginning to fill it up. " I'll promise you even your Cousin Adelaide won't dare keep this from your mother ! Even if you're right and she is ill, it's a fool's idea to keep Billy's danger from her ; and I'll tell Mrs. Sinclair so, too. There "—he added two words with frowning energy—" I'll send that down by the car that's bringing my colleague up from the station, and you'll see it will do better than those letters Mrs. Addington never gets ! What's that, Rose ? "

Rose, red-eyed, stood in the doorway, brought down for one minute from her endless watch over Billy.

" I guess there's one letter Mrs. Addington's got," she returned, harshly, " and that's from me. I wrote to her three days ago, and enclosed the letter to young Johnston Earlwood. And I told him too, good and strong, that Billy's ma had got to know he mightn't get no better ; and I bet she does—by now ! "

" But we hadn't Johnston's address," cried Nan, wildly

Rose sniffed, scornfully. " You hadn't," she retorted, absently. " Doctor, please come right up to Billy. He—my land, who's *this* ? "

She whirled, staring, at a quiet-faced man who had come in silently from the front hall, but for once she said nothing to Nan's whispered answer. Nor, miracle of miracles for Rose, did she even open her mouth when Dr. Marsh's night telegram had gone, and he and the specialist had shut the door of Billy's room on her and Nan, except when snatching in the boiling water and sterilized towels that one or the other had always ready for Dr. Marsh's quick hand. When that business was over, Rose cried where she sat on the stairs by Nan—Nan, who was long past tears. And not till two in the morning did Dr. Marsh appear to look over the banisters.

"Billy's better," he said, quietly. "Do you hear me? Only wants food and nursing now, and that he'll get, I know. Coffee and sandwiches, Rose, please. And then get to bed to be fresh for the morning. The doctor and I will finish out the night."

Nan declared afterwards that Rose hugged the strange doctor before he left next morning, but his directions left the pair staring at each other where they stood beside Billy—a new Billy, sleeping as he had not slept for days.

"Oysters, cream, beef-tea, jelly; Billy's to have all of 'em," Rose whispered, heavily,

" and thirty-five cents all we got in the house, and your ma never runs bills ! "

" She needn't now," said Nan, calmly. " I'll go out and get everything for Billy. I'm going to sell the Crown Derby bowl. That lady who started the new Woman's Exchange down in the village told mother she'd give her twenty-five dollars for it any day."

" What ? " Rose would have shrieked if it had not been for Billy. " That old china bowl Billy had for a crown on the idol the day your cousin first come here ? Why, your ma's had it for years—and I don't believe it would fetch twenty-five cents. I don't believe in that Woman's Exchange either. I never saw any cake in their window I'd be hired to eat. And your ma might be real mad, too ! "

" She won't ; not for Billy ! And I'll go down and sell the bowl to the Exchange." Nan's mouth set as she slid out of Billy's room to put on her coat and hat, and stayed set while she wrapped up the Crown Derby bowl. She dared not begin bills, with the unreliable Fielding for her only source of ready money to pay them. Cousin Adelaide might send her the money, perhaps ; but Nan's faith in Cousin Adelaide was shaken. " If even Rose's wages have never come, besides no answers to my letters, it means I've just got to sell the bowl," she thought, desperately.

She flung open the front door, with the doomed bowl under her arm, and stood checked, paralysed, on the veranda.

Mr. Perry Earlwood, Johnston's father, who had sent her the books on fruit-farming that she had never used, was coming up the path to the house—huge in a fur overcoat, and pulling fur motor gloves off his stiff hands!

CHAPTER XVIII

" MOTHER."

NAN'S heart almost stopped beating.

There was one thing—only one—that could have brought Johnston's father all the way from New York in the car that stood by the gate. Something must have happened to Mother!

" Mother ! " Nan gasped, as if no other word would come out of her where she stood motionless on the doorstep. " Is mother——"

Mr. Perry Earlwood seemed to reach her in one second, and have a furry arm round her and her bowl.

" Mother's all right," he said, sharply. " She's well. She's been ill, but she's all over it, and she's coming home to-morrow by rail in my private car, with Johnston and Lil. Now tell me "—he looked down at the small pinched face against his fur coat, and Nan little knew he was afraid to go on—" how's the boy ? "

" Better," but she clutched him dizzily with

the hand that was free of the wrapped-up bowl. " Only Mother, Mr. Earlwood ; I can't understand ! Why didn't I ever hear from Mother ? "

" I'll tell you," returned Mr. Earlwood. Somehow Nan found herself listening to all he had to say from the big chair in the living-room, with Mr. Earlwood shutting the door and poking the fire as if he were not a magnate at all, but only a boy like Dick. " You didn't hear from your mother because she had to go to a nursing-home, quick, to be operated on for appendicitis ; your cousin and her maid went with her ; Lil closed the flat and went to my wife, and a half-baked new janitor put all their letters and telegrams into the letter-box of their empty apartment, instead of handing them in to the office."

" But why didn't Lil—somebody—find out ? "

" Nobody ever went down "—dryly—" till I went myself yesterday. Your cousin had telephoned to the Rosedale Apartments Office every morning for letters, and there never were any, but nobody seemed to have thought of asking the janitor. Mrs. Sinclair was pretty worried about your mother, and Lil seems to have been frantic most of the time, so neither of them——" He bit back that neither Lil nor

16

Cousin Adelaide seemed ever to have given a thought to Nan and Billy, and that it was for Nan's and Billy's sake and no other that he himself had come. "It's all well that ends well," he concluded, rather sharply. "Your mother wouldn't have you told about her operation for fear you'd worry, and of course they told her you were all right—till yesterday, when I had to take her up all the bunch of letters you'd sent. Then we'd have had to tie her down if I hadn't happened to be coming this way myself."

"But Dr. Marsh's telegram?" Nan gasped. "About the specialist?"

"Never heard of it. D'ye mean you had a specialist?"

But he nodded when he heard the specialist's verdict.

"Sensible girl to let him come! Now, you and I have to see that Billy gets all the nourishment he can take, and a pinched looking girl I could name, too. You make a list and I'll do messenger boy and buy the stuff. What's that?" as Nan murmured something in a shamefaced way. "Oh, money! Don't want any money—that's all right. What's that you were taking out with you when I came?" —with sudden suspicion.

" Only a bowl," but Nan's tired face reddened. " It's for—for the Woman's Exchange."

" You poor, valiant little monkey," was what Mr. Earlwood thought. What he said was : " I wouldn't worry about bowls now. Oysters, you said, and——"

But Nan interrupted as he scrawled with a gold pencil in a Russia leather book.

" But I don't understand yet how *you* knew about Billy. I—Mr. Earlwood, how did you happen to come ? "

" Oh, that ! " Mr. Perry Earlwood wrote his last word and shut up the book. " That's simple. Only, why in the world, Nan, didn't you write to me yourself ? "

" Write to you ? I wouldn't have dared ! " Nan stared at him. " I never thought of it."

" Then it's as well someone in this house has some sense," Mr. Earlwood returned, coolly. He pulled a somewhat remarkable looking letter out of his pocket, with a white label off a brown paper parcel glued on to it instead of a written address, and Nan jumped.

" My goodness—*Rose*! " she gasped. " But —oh, Mr Earlwood, she told me she had written to *Johnston*, and I never gave it another thought. I never would have let her write to you ! "

" Well, she didn't, exactly. But Perry

Johnston Earlwood is me, if it's Johnston too.
And as his letters don't usually come to my
office, especially addressed with my private
label that I happened to have put on a certain
parcel myself—" his eyes twinkled at Nan,—
" well, naturally I opened it.   I was away when
it arrived, or I'd have been here before.   That
Rose, whoever she is, has sense ! "

"What did she say ? "

" Plain language "—dryly. " ' Mr. Earlwood,
Billy's dying. Tell his ma to come or we can't
save him.   Yors respectful, Rose at Mrs.
Addington's.' "

Nan gulped.   But Mr. Earlwood's large
hand fell on her shoulder.

" Never weep over past fusses, Nan," said
he, calmly. " Doesn't pay. I'll be back in
an hour or so from the village, and you sit
still till I come. Hi, stop ! Where are you
going ? "

" To tell Rose mother's coming. I forgot
her—and it's been all her ! "

" Well, don't yell it ! There'll be plenty of
time to tell Billy when he wakes up," returned
her adviser, practically. But he turned a
queer eye on Nan as she flew out of the room.
" The poor little soul," said he, thoughtfully.
" But I'm glad I put a stopper on her mother

coming down with me—there's no need for her
to see that child till she's fed ! "

Fed Nan certainly was : when Mr. Perry
Earlwood undertook a thing he did it. Oysters,
hot soup, jellies—" The whole stock of that
Woman's Exchange—and the things ain't near
so bad as I expected," as Rose commented
with grudging awe—arrived with him in his car.
Furthermore, he sent Rose and Nan to bed,
and he himself kept watch by Billy all the long
afternoon, as knowledgeably and gently as any
woman. And whether it was the magnetism of
his easy strength, or the doses of beef-tea he
administered between Billy's exhausted sleeps,
Dr. Marsh found the little boy miraculously
better.

" Now, all he wants is his mother, and she'll
be here in the morning," Mr. Perry Earlwood
informed the jubilant Rose. " I've told him,
and he's going to sleep, like a good boy, till she
comes. I'll be off to the hotel now, and take
a rest." He yawned widely, having in sober
truth left New York towards midnight the night
before.

" But you'll be up again ?   I'll see you before
you go ? " Nan seized him as he shrugged
himself into his fur coat down in the hall.

" My time's worth a pearl a minute," Mr.

Earlwood grinned cheerfully. " But I'm going to give you two pearls' worth in the morning—all to yourself, though you didn't use my fruit-farming books. I'll be up with your mother when the morning train gets in."

But when he did come, with Mrs. Addington and Lil beside him in the tonneau of his big car, and Johnston in front by the chauffeur, Nan hardly looked at him. Her mother was back—white, tired, but shining-eyed as she kissed Nan over and over.

" Oh, Nan, and Rose," she said, as that faithful servant laughed and cried in the background, " I can't ever repay you. If Billy had died—oh, I never could have forgiven myself and Adelaide for not having made sure that my letters came to me ! "

" Well, he ain't dying ; he's quite perky," Rose began, stoutly, and suddenly sobbed : " We done our best, we done our best."

" And you'll keep on doing it," Mr. Perry Earlwood commanded abruptly. " Get Mrs. Addington some hot soup or something. And, Mrs. Addington, you take my arm, and I'll go upstairs with you to Billy."

What Mrs. Addington said and what Billy said Mr. Perry Earlwood told to no one. He left the two, Billy in his mother's arms where she sat on his bed, and looked for some time out of the hall window, before he remembered that he had to get back to New York, and that if his time was worth a pearl a minute he wanted to give some of it to Nan.

" H—m," said he, and descended slowly to the living-room. But in the doorway he stopped thoughtfully.

Nan stood in the middle of it, staring at Lil, in new furs ; then, suddenly, from her to Johnston Earlwood. Life had been a hazy dream to her since Billy had been so ill, but something in the look of Lil and Johnston suddenly made her remember why her mother had gone to New York.

" My goodness, Lil," she blurted, with her usual calm tactlessness, " I forgot ! What on earth did you do about Tony Yelverton ? "

Lil turned scarlet. Johnston Earlwood began to laugh.

" He's gone west, Nan," he returned, with his eyes twinkling. " And he's not likely t be back for some time."

" Oh," said Nan, and looked at Lil again. " Then——"

Johnston nodded. " Would you mind if Li married *me*, Nan ? " he inquired.

" I don't like her marrying anyone," returned

the candid Nan. " But—oh, if Billy gets well,
I can put up with *anything* ! "

Mr. Perry Earlwood, at the living-room door
burst into a loud chuckle as Rose, passing him
with a tray of coffee and hot biscuits, dropped
it suddenly on the nearest table.

" You're wanting to marry Lil ! " she
exclaimed, once more the directress of the
establishment and perfectly oblivious of
Johnston's father in the doorway. " Well, she's
all right ; but Miss Nan's the best of 'em,
though it's no good my saying so. When
children—boys especially—is set on having one
toy in the toyshop, it's no use to tell 'em the
paint comes off. You've just got to let them
have it and find out for themselves ! "

" I bet Lil's paint won't come off," Johnston
rejoined, calmly. " And Nan wouldn't have
me, Rose."

" Rose, you're horrid ! " Lil burst out furiously.

" Am I ? I guess it's what you call reaction,"
Rose returned smartly. " Nan and me have
been sitting by a death-bed all these days,
worrying because your ma didn't know about
it, and thinking we'd never save Billy. And
we wouldn't have, I don't believe, if it hadn't
been for Nan sitting beside him, and singing

to him what he calls his ' brave hymn ' when he couldn't sleep : brave as brave herself, and me couldn't speak for choking. I ain't cross with you, Miss Lil, and I'm glad you're going to be happy ; but I'm so relieved your ma's come that I've got to be snappy to someone, just to let the steam off. Talk about getting rewarded for troubles in this world—your ma's here, and Mr. Earlwood's give me a present big enough to start an account in the savings bank. He—my land, Mr. Earlwood, I forgot you was there ! "

" Hear, hear," said Mr. Earlwood, advancing from the doorway as Rose fled abashed. " Now, Lil, you and Johnston make yourselves scarce. I want to speak to Nan, and then I must be off."

" You've been an angel to me, and to Rose, too," Nan said, rather unsteadily, as the other two followed Rose. " Have some soup Rose has brought for you before you go."

" Never eat between meals ; " but he helped himself to a large cupful. " Now, look here, Nan, I've something to tell you ; and you go and repeat all I've said to your mother, and tell her I'll write it all to her later. There's a company who are thinking of building a new railroad from here to New York instead of your old scrap-heap, and linking on from here to the line from Boston."

" How horrid," Nan interrupted, hastily. " Why, we'll just turn into a town ! "

" Yes ? You wait a bit "—calmly. " You want to go to college, and I don't suppose you'd like your mother to work all her life. And this new railroad company "——He paused to glance at Nan, silent, and suddenly breathless, before he nodded affirmatively to something in her face. " Yes, you've got it ! The company has bought up a good deal of land round here, and now they're going to offer your mother her own price—that I'll set for her—for all the pasture and the woodland above your house, where they want to have the station for the new line. Understand, Miss Nan ? "

But for a long minute Nan was speechless. Her mother would never have to work any more, nor sell strawberries and vegetables to a grocer who did not pay her, could keep Rose, could send Billy to a good school—and suddenly it all broke out of her.

" It's you—it's all you." She flew straight to Mr. Earlwood, and clutched the big coat that he was struggling into. " I don't know why you've done it, but even you don't know what it means. Mother's saved! As long as she lives she'll never have to wash one single other dish, nor sweep, nor anything hard. And—oh, do you think Billy can go to Groton? I know it's late to put his name down."

" I expect so." Mr. Earlwood looked down at her oddly. He could have said he had perhaps hurried his railroad for the sake of a girl whom he had once advised to take dress-making lessons, when he found her crying over a scarlet picture of a dancer, alone on a disused road, and for whom he had felt oddly responsible ever since. But he merely chuckled down at her shining eyes. " What about a girl who wanted to go to college? "

Nan did her best breakdown all round him. " That too," she said, stopping breathless. " Oh, Mr. Earlwood, Billy always called Johnston ' the Magnet,' and I believe it's true, because he's drawn us to you. And I never " —she flushed guiltily—" never used those fruit-farming books either."

" H—m," said " the Magnet's " father, dryly. "' I don't know that I ever really thought you were cut out for fruit-farming, Nan. Now you get along and tell all I've told you to your mother ; and good-bye. I'll be along in the spring, when that railroad begins to go through."

Billy, lying contented in his bed, wondered why his mother and Nan and Lil and Johnston were all holding hands there suddenly, and laughing.

" It's a railroad—a new one," said Nan, breaking away to kiss him. " You can be an ' aigine ' driver, Billy, when you're well."

" Don't see any railroad," said Billy, quite sturdily. " 'Spects anything can't matter— now mother's come home ! "

Printed by Publishers' Graphics Canada